Wizardry of Insights

Flairs and Glairs

Publication House

"Wizardry of Insights"

ISBN No: " 978-93-90799-61-9"
1ˢᵗ Edition
Language – English and Hindi

Flairs and Glairs
Publication House
Regd. Under MSME Act.

Disclaimer

This is a work of fiction and solely represent the thoughts of the corresponding authors of the articles. Our editors have tried their best to edit the content of all the authors and check the plagiarism.

All the write-ups in this book are unique and are only published in this book.

In case any plagiarism or error is found, only the author is responsible alone, and not the publisher or the Compilers.

Cover Designing and Book Formatting
Shubham Shah and Ishani Agarwal

About the book

The WIZARDRY OF INSIGHTS is an assortment of insights of co-authors all over India in the form of short stories, open letters and poetries.

Each writer has penned down their insights in such a way that you will feel captivated, enchanted, happy and experience paradise of words. These writers have used their writing as sorcery to enchant their point of view into your subconscious mind.

The main reason behind the publication of this anthology is to share experiences and diverse perspectives of people towards situations in life and to provide a platform for all emerging writers to exhibit their talent.

Acknowledgement

The creation of this anthology would not have been possible without the co-authors. Their insights made this anthology a magical one. Thank you co-authors, without your support and insights this anthology wouldn't be magical.

Thanks to everyone who has tried sincerely and has put forth attempts for this treasury to be a triumph.

Above all, hearty thanks to my family and friends for supporting us throughout this anthology. I am thankful to Flairs and Glairs Publication without whom this project wouldn't have been possible.

Lastly, I thank the almighty for giving me this opportunity and solidarity to complete this anthology successfully.

Co Author

Shubham Shah (Founder Flairs and Glairs)
Ishani Agarwal (Co-Founder Flairs and Glairs)

1. Vaishni Venkatesh (Chief of wizards)
2. Akshaya Vamsikrishnan
3. Sonia.V
4. Ajay T
5. Geetha Priya A
6. Damini A
7. Uzaifa Fathima M
8. Harshini Jayachandran
9. Supriya.c.s.k
10. Gowthami J
11. Janani J
12. Suveetha
13. Santhosh Pandian A
14. Sirushtika R S
15. Swathi Nandakumar
16. Vashcini js
17. Divya K
18. Samyuktha S
19. Sasikala V
20. Moneshasree J
21. A P Rabhina Roy
22. A.K. Pratibha
23. Vasanth N
24. Ramya Prabhakaran

25. Rajeshwari Elango
26. Sharon Hrithika S
27. Shakina M P
28. Jayashree S
29. Babithashree S
30. Bertina S
31. Subiksa V
32. Pooja
33. Vidhyasri K
34. Nivedha Balamurugan
35. Manjari Balamurugan
36. Swetha Pillai
37. Preethi L
38. Surudhi Rajasekaran
39. Sri Vaishnavi P
40. Vinoth M
41. Sriram Chidambaram Ilangovan
42. Shwetaa S H
43. Sarah Dawn Jebalance
44. Surander S M
45. Priyadharshini Kumar
46. Gunadharshini C
47. Lucya immaculate M
48. Janani Kannan
49. Haritha Baskar
50. Oviyapriya K
51. Anjali Gaur

Shubham Shah

(Founder- Flairs and Glairs)

Shubham Shah, an entrepreneur at "Flairs & Glairs" a brand with dynamics in events organizing and cultural educational pan INDIA, is a 26yrs old guy who recently has entered the digital platform of imprinting emotions. He has initiated with his own open mic platform to help budding poets and aspiring writers under his brand named as "Teekhe Zasbaaat"

He is a commerce graduate from the Bhagalpur City of Bihar. He states Writing has impersonated him since childhood and he has now been writing for over a decade!

Cooking, on the other hand, is his passion! He also mentions, trying out new things just tickles him!

When asked sir, Why SPICY EMOTIONS?

He smiled and added, "agar jasbaat teekhe na ho toh wo jasbaat kahan" Spices are all that blends! So do his words!

As a chef, he presents to you his dish! Hot and freshly served! Taste it! Feel it! Enjoy it! You can also find his writing in the Book "Teekhe Zasbaaat" and 50+ Co-authored anthologies. With his passion to explore opportunities across Platforms, he is working with keen devotion and We wish him all the very best for his future ventures.

He is Featured in the **International Magazine De-Mode** for his upcoming solo novel.

He is **Approved by Ne8x for its Lit Fest,** and is a **Golden Star Awards 2020 Winner.**

He is an **India Book of Records Holder** for his Anthology **Satrang,** and has the **Grandmaster** title by **Asia Book of Records**, for the same.

He has also been featured in **Prabhat Khabar**, **Dainik Jagran** and other renowned Newspaper for his achievements. He has also been awarded with **India Star Republic Award 2021.**

He has been a proud co-author to

India Book of Records (Title- Black)

World Book of Records (Title -15 Wonders of Poetries)

India Book of Records (Title - Aaina)

Vajra World Records Holder (Title - Gustakhi Maaf Hai)

High Range of Records Holder (Title - Gustakhi Maaf Hai)

Share your reviews on his

INSTAGRAM

        @spicy_emotions
        @shubham4shah

Or via email on

        shubham2shah@gmail.com

To stay tuned to his work and opportunities follow his business Handles

INSTAGRAM   FACEBOOK   YOUTUBE

        @flairsandglairs
        @teekhezasbaaat

WEBSITE:

        https://flairsandglairs.in/
        https://flairsandglairs.com/

Ishani Agarwal

(Co-Founder- Flairs and Glairs)

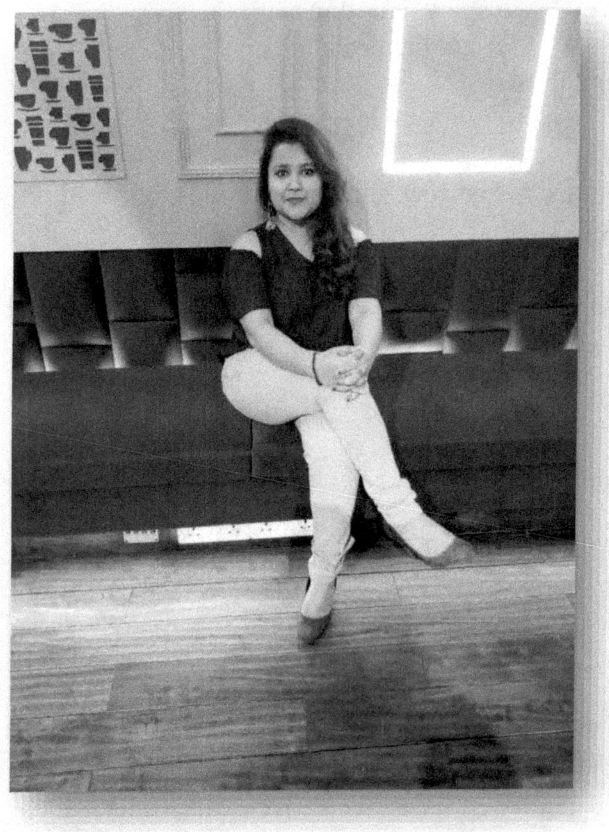

Ishani Agarwal hails from the City of Joy, Kolkata.
She is the co-founder of her Community "Teekhe Zasbaaat" and Flairs and Glairs Publication.
Been a Compiler for 45+ Anthologies, she is in the process for more. Co-authored in 150+ Anthologies. She is a India Book of Records Holder, a Vajra World Records Holder, a High Range of Records Holder and a Bravo Record holder.

Approved by Ne8x for its Lit Fest 2020, and Literary Icon 2020. Also a Golden Star Awards Winner 2020.
She has also been awarded with India Star Republic Award 2021.
She has been featured by the National Magazine "Taree Zameen Par" with the title 'unstoppable'.
Also featured in the International Magazine DeMode for her upcoming solo novel, she is proud to write on social issues, and is happy with the love she is receiving.
Connect with her on Instagram: @Ishani_agarwal_quotes / @compilations_so_far

VAISHNI VENKATESH
(COMPILER)

Vaishni Venkatesh is a witty marketer. Electronic and Instrumentation engineer by profession currently pursuing MBA focused in Marketing & HR. Born and brought up in Chennai.

She is a motivational speaker who is ambitious and charismatic. She has been a resource person and speaker for many events, seminars, open mics, and also the MC of several events. She has grown out to be reckoned with confidence and liveliness personified on stage.

She is curious in nature with a high eagerness to learn new things. She believes that kindness will conquer the world. She draws a solution for every problem beautifully on her wrist. She loves to write because she reach people through her writing, aiming to be a changemaker.

She enjoys sharing knowledge and guiding everyone towards their goals. She contributes her active participation in volunteering and social service. She is a person who believes that ultimate purpose of life is not achieving only one's goal but to help the needy as much as possible.

She is passionate about research, digital marketing, writing books, compiling anthologies & being co-author in anthologies as well. She is also experienced in event management and event organizing. She has her own food blog with mouthwatering recipes, and reviews.

Apart from being a topper in both her UG & PG, she is interested in doodling, new language learning, blogging and being a foodie forever.

Instagram ID: vaishni_venkatesh
Instagram ID: lafoodbinge

LONESOME

I figured time would fix it, or companions or work or family doubtlessly would, yet they did close to assist me with suffering it. I diverted, sedated, deluded myself to shake the emotions, yet it developed inside me like the forest fire. At the same time, I have been lonely for the duration of my life. Still, I do not have the foggiest idea about the reason behind this why. I have battled it like a detested enemy. I evaded it like disgraceful memories. Memories that are always to be closed in a box. I attempted to deal with it like a mystery infection. I wrote in my journal with all pages loaded up with ink that is not visible.

My whole life spent in one interest to quit being desolate. To discover a fix to this old toxin, this feeling of being ousted from somewhere perfect, somewhere I had a place and originated. A spot whose each memory was cleaned from me, leaving behind just the sourceless throb. And I do not know why it took me years to understand I am not different. We all encounter this period of being lonely in various phases of our life. We appear as stones cast with a spell and tossed into inhumane oceans. We as a whole are confronting and going through a similar low feel, and vanishing profound, together or isolated yet totally too far.

Furthermore, we have no clue about that for what reason did we land this way. We never knew the reason behind this WHY! Something is absent from everything and keeping us inadequate. I found that loneliness is the piece left missing purposefully from the riddles of our life. The void that makes seekers of us, whether we feel and realize it or not, is the absence we need to fill. Our soul clarion call, it is the place where the words continue moving, it is where the art begins, it is the point where you concentrate on your success and reach it if you use this loneliness in the right manner.

Through the entirety of my self-duplicities, egocentrism, implosion, the lonesome feel was the one, in particular, that endured. Through all the pain, only this remained. Finally, I began to confront that lonesome was the voice I needed to figure out. If I am the flower, it is the fragrance. In my smugness, it is my wrath. I would have remained as a side character, but it carried me to this stage. Without this lonesome feel, I couldn't ever have persevered. All my latent capacity would have stayed in profound quiet, and I couldn't ever have changed the entire story into success forever and would have remained in the cage.

My honest muse, my guiding divine, I learned, at last, we were made lonely by design. So it is never off-base to be lonely. It helps us to identify our flaws, the people of our life, and the ones who always stand with us. It is the best magical spell executing the perfect magic with sparkle everywhere.

AKSHAYA VAMSIKRISHNAN

Akshaya Vamsikrishnan is born in Andhra Pradesh and settled in Chennai, currently pursuing MBA. She is a jovial and friendly character who loves to take care of animals. She is passionate about singing. She is interested in music and a few sports. She is a person who is concerned about doing social activities. She likes to write contents rarely. She loves to explore and learn new things.

Instagram ID: __idhaya_rani__

BELIEVE

What do you think is necessary for success? Is it about people's thoughts on you? Or is it about what people think you can and can't do? There are three main necessities to achieve success in life! Without these, you can't reach even a bit near to success.

Firstly, BELIEVE in YOURSELF! Yes it's the first necessity. What happens when you don't believe in yourself?! You won't be able to think, plan or create mindmaps about how you're going to achieve your goal.
  "The more you believe in yourself, the more you could trust yourself. The more you trust yourself, the less you compare yourself to others!"

Secondly, it's your EFFORTS! When you start believing in yourself, you tend to see ways in which you should do something in order to achieve success. Only by putting efforts to achieve your goal, you can grow towards it. The more efforts and hardwork you put in, the more you feel satisfied about where you're going in your path of success.

 "One important key to success is self- confidence. An important key to self- confidence is preparation!"

Finally, it's your PATIENCE! After putting in all your efforts, you wait untill you see the final result of what you had been aiming for. If not you do more and more to compensate to reach your goal. The only thing in this process of believing yourself that you should NEVER DO is GIVING UP!!

One thing that must be taken care in this process is that you must not duplicate any successful personality rather always be yourself and have trust and faith in yourself!

SONIA V

Sonia is from Chennai, She is a B.E student, a social activist. Her goal is to become an entrepreneur. She is an optimistic person. She exhibits her best in art works, web designing, gardening. she always try to give her level best in each and everything she does.

Instagram ID: Me._.sonia_

HOPE ON PLANET EARTH

We all inevitably face struggles in our lives . Sometimes it would become challenging to face on our own; a simple hopeful thought will help us to get through it. Let me give you some more clarity about hope. Now visualize yourself lost in a deep darkness. You can't move anywhere without any further instruction, you don't know how long the path goes on, you don't know whether will you be able to find a way out of it; while you are wondering, you heard a voice whispering 'step forward'. Now you are waiting for the next command, again a voice whispered saying 'run straight up to 10 counts'. Now you might have been doubtful that how in this dreadful darkness I can be able to find a way by following the silly instructions, but you did it unmindfully in order to get out of it somehow. You were waiting for the next command for upto 30 mins, earlier you received the command very next instant of completion, but now you are waiting on and on. You couldn't find any whisper. As I said before without any further instructions you can't move further. So now as a mankind we lose our patience and give up on that, we lose hope and think that our life ends up there tucked in a deep darkness. Now stop your imagination and come back to reality now what if I say that it is 798 sq.ft hall which has a door in the state of closed .Now you might think if I had the patience to wait for some more while, the instruction would have come and I would have been successfully coming out of the darkness. But that's not the thing which made the voice disappear its because of the doubtful thought that you had before which makes the whole circumstance a failure even it has the way nearer. "Hope is being able to see that there is light despite all of the darkness". Your problems are like the darkness; the voice is the hope, if you hope on yourself undoubtfully without giving up on any circumstances then you will definitely be successful in some way.
"Hope makes things magical, that makes things real and it is all I consider to exist."

AJAY T

Ajay is from Chennai, He has completed his B.E.(Mechanical) form Panimalar Engineering College, And currently pursuing his M.B.A.(Marketing & Operation) from St. Joseph's college of Engineering. He like to paint, and fantasizes about wild animals . He's a better friend who cares a lot about other's than him self's, and kind hearted person and trust everyone more.

Instagram ID: Ajay Buster

SELFLESS

Let's think why shouldn't we must be selfish in our life let's consider a simple example you are working in an office and you are the team leader and you have a human resource higher official . In a case if your team member wants a help from you but if you do that he would be well recognized in the organization due to his improved skill hence you refuse to do that . why doesn't the same thought comes from your human resource higher official which leads to no growth in the organization. And you have to create a demand in order to get promoted to the next level here you require an assurance. This demand leads to business which will leads to spending all your earning hence the cycle repeats. So, if you are selfless you would help someone without any expectations thus chain will carry over to others and in some point of time if you require some help. You would receive it from some unexpected place or person due to the selfless act of other's you don't have to do big things in order to completely help the needy you could do the at most part that you could do in order to help them this builds a confidence inside them. Let see in another point of view if you go to worship god to the respective places you will pray for an help at this place the god will help you with out any expectation in return. He / She is also a selfless person who is praised by most of them .

One of the greatest selfless person well known by all is Dr. A. P. J. Abdul kalam also known as the "missile man of India" he is the good example for what we get for being selfless that is what everyone seeks for " Recognition" so be selfless at all part of time and let the chain carry on through others.

GEETHA PRIYA A

Geetha Priya is from Chennai, currently residing in Tiruvotiyur. She is a schoolgirl studying 12th standard in Our lady's High School. Besides being a topper girl, she likes to sing, dance, listening to music. Geetha always wants to read anybody by their mind. So, she was decided to do her higher studies in psychology. Her dream was to make her signature to the autograph.

LEAD YOUR LIFE WITH HAPPINESS

Here, I wish to begin the writing with a beautiful story, I heard one day, so the story goes something like this, one day, A teacher wanted to demonstrate something to her students so she gave each student a balloon and had everyone write their own name on it, not knowing what she was about to do or say. They excitedly did it anyway.

Each student wrote their name on that balloon and handed it back to the teacher. Then the teacher took all the balloons and put them in the other room then she told them that they were going to go in that room and try to find the balloon with their name on it within five minutes. They quickly got up and ran to the room pretty soon everything was chaotic, all of the students were frantically looking for their own balloon. They were pushing each other and everyone was getting frustrated and angry. But nobody could find their own balloon. Then the teacher asks everyone to just collect a random balloon and tells them to give it to the person whose name was written on it. Pretty soon, "Everyone had their own balloon". I think that this story is a great metaphor for life because this is what happens to us. We constantly look for happiness not knowing where it is and we never realize that it is within us. Happiness lies within ourselves and our desire to help others and be happy. When you give them their happiness, as soon as you will get your own happiness and this is what life is all about. It's not just to help others by giving money and some things which they need, even a consoling word is enough for them. So, search your happiness in helping others.

DAMINI A

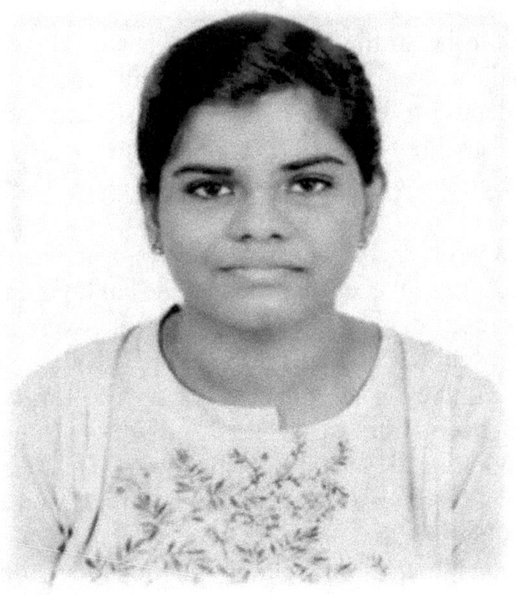

A passionate young writer, who likes to experiment in every genre!
An ambivert who loves being creative!
And a Constant believer of 'Love yourself more'
Instagram ID: dams__541

WRATH

Wrath, a sin born in hell.
Rage of a crestfallen human.
A feral expression to a squall.
The mask of our suppressed fear,
Harping poisonous smear.

Wrath, the best friend of Pride and Envy.
Rudiment of grudge and heart's peavy.
Aliment to kedge our vainglory.
The only boon, its ephemeral clutch,
Hatching us to a demonic apery.

Wrath, the battle where words are weapons,
Rearing our vengeance with gore.
Aftermath bestow us, a rueful eagre
To our soulful haven;
Heaping us, the impiety of Heaven.

Wrath, the self-injecting poison for
Renege of temporisers.
And giving a wistful smile
To those sycophants filled with bile,
Hushing us up, for a baneful exile.

Wrath, Oh! the soul's woe for
Repugnant repudiation and remorse.
Alas! It never neglects evermore friends,
Tampering their memories and faith.
Hew them, they sprout as two gorse.

Wrath, the asperity teaches us,
Rekindling hope leads to dander.
A learning lesson from it, it's you,
The trouble and the peace, it's you,
Hitch and the solution, it's you!

UZAIFA FATHIMA M

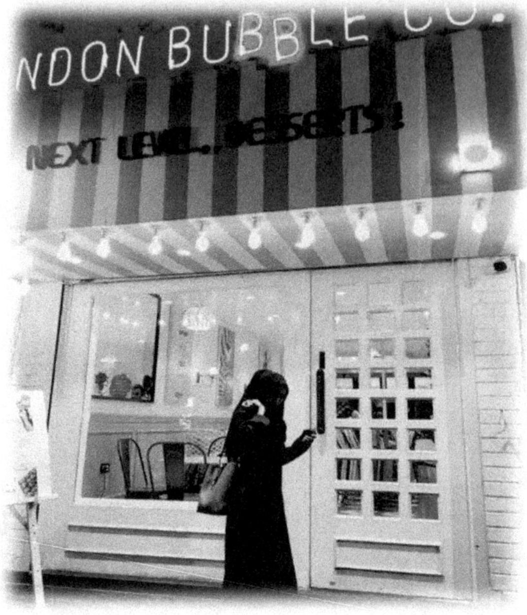

Uzaifa Fathima M is born and brought up in Chennai. She loves nature and fun loving girl. She is interested in sports and games too. She loves adventure in life and also she is concern about treating others with respect and giving her the same. She has lot of faith, courage, and to be RESPECT.

HELPING HANDS

"You have to give respect to get respect."

Lauren Barnholdt.

Let's go through a few things happening around us in our society. People who are uneducated been working as helping hands for us but not as salves. They are working at construction place, maidservant/housekeeper, peon(hospitals, schools, colleges, etc.,) farmers, garbage cleaner, Auto driver and many more. They're the daily breadwinners.

"Proper respect for others is the most prudent rule to directing the measure of reverence due to ourselves."

In my personal experience, they have the faith, courage and determination to survive in daily life. They have family waiting for them for food to eat and survive in the world of internet but not for the luxury living. The living of life is arduous and awful yet they are strong enough to face the other day of sunrise.

They aren't treated well in the majority. Even they have children to care for, husband/wife to look after, parents waiting for them who are old enough and have no money for the right treatment they need, Besides they have the beautiful smile on the face, they believe in miracles.

"Believe in yourself, let's bring a change and little can make a big difference."

•	To the auto drivers - after dropping us safe in our destination let's say "thank you" respect them with uncle.

•	To maidservant- Hear out to them about what they say. If we get our hands together and do this and can also do more but this is enough for them to bring a smile on their face.

"The smile is worth a thousand words"

They also dream of success, where they think,

"Without struggle, success has no value"

"True happiness lies in giving it to others"
                                    -Indian Proverb.

HARSHINI JAYACHANDRAN

Harshini Jayachandran, an aspiring engineer pursuing Electronics and Instrumentation engineering, is an amateur writer who has just started attempting writing anthologies. Her epigram towards writing is an iterate by Benjamin Franklin, "Either write something worth reading, or do something worth writing".

Instagram ID: _.harshini._._

SAGACITY ON CHARACTER ASSASSINATION

What aspect of an individual addresses the true nature, whether good or bad of that particular individual? Yes, it's definitely the individual's character. And what if that individual's character is portrayed in a wrong way, so that it affects the image of the individual?

In the modern times a person's character is usually judged based on the following: Honesty, reliability, trustworthiness, capability to control emotions like anger etc; humbleness and so on. Sometimes it may be misjudged and who bares all the loss when a person's character is misjudged, it's only that particular person whose character is assassinated in his/her surroundings or work place, which leads him/her into immense mental pressure and stress, which he/she often fails in handling.

"They can't kill the truth, so they try to assassinate the character"

My acuity on Character attacks:

This concept of Character assassination has many synonyms associated to it some of them are personal-attack, ad hominem, smear campaign, aspersion, calumny, defamation, denigration, detraction, scandal and slander. Character assassination is the attempted ruin of

reputation. For instance, George W Bush, former US President, was demonized over his cavalier attitude towards warfare. Techniques used to assassinate an individual's character need not be true always; An accusation of wrong-doing is more than enough to sow the seeds of doubts and false conception in the minds of others. The psychological effect of Character assassination attacks may result in a wide range of negative emotional trauma which influence an individual's mood and his/her immediate decisions and emotional states which affect the individual's reputation, relationships and

lifestyle. Character assassination what a wonderful concept it is!, Ordinary assassination works only at that instance, but this idea works every single day. This concept of Character assassination results in psychological traumas in the minds of those undergoing it. So better, Make a habit of shutting down conversations that aim to make others feel low. Character assassination is not fun anymore. People who have a habit of destroying others character should be punished badly. Martin Luther King once said, "Darkness cannot drive out darkness, Only light can do that; Hate cannot drive out hate, only love can do that; So let's spread love and positivity every way possible instead of destructing one's character and being engine failure in a ship for them to drown into the ocean of negativity.

SUPRIYA C S K

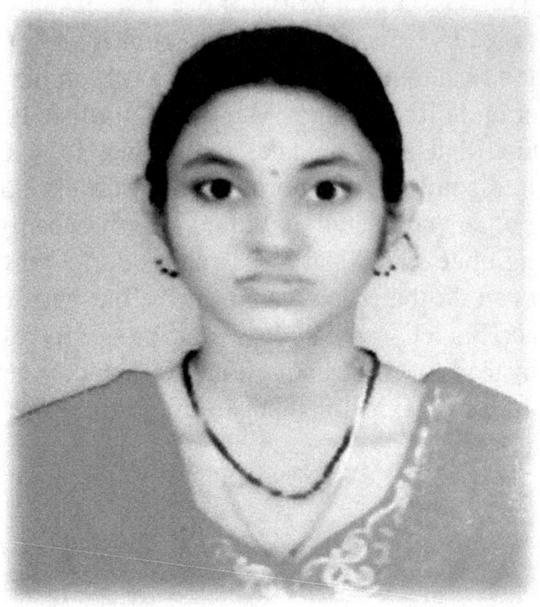

As a writer in person Supriya is always a dreamer and a creative writer as well . She is always in a process of searching herself and finding something new every time .
Instagram ID: csksupriya

HISS OF SILENCE

Hello darkness, my old friend
I've come to talk with you again
Because a vision softly creeping
Left its seeds while I was sleeping
And the vision that was planted in my brain
Still remains
Within the sound of silence
In restless dreams I walked alone
Narrow streets of cobblestone
'Beneath the halo of a street lamp
I turned my collar to the cold and damp
When my eyes were stabbed by the flash of a neon light
That split the night
And touched the sound of silence
And in the naked light, I saw
Ten thousand people, maybe more
People talking without speaking
People hearing without listening
People writing songs that voices never share
And no one dared
Disturb the sound of silence
"Fools", said I, "You do not know
Silence like a cancer grows
Hear my words that I might teach you
Take my arms that I might reach you"
But my words, like silent raindrops fell
And echoed
In the wells of silence
And the people bowed and prayed
To the neon god they made
And the sign flashed out its warning
In the words that it was forming

And the sign said, "The words of the prophets are written on
the subway walls
And tenement halls"
And whispered in the sound of silence.

GOWTHAMI J

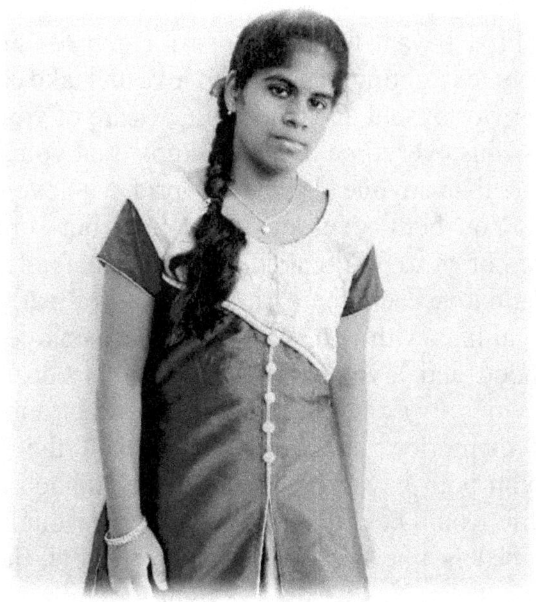

Gowthami Jayapal born in Chennai, currently studying 12th std (Biology group). She passion to become a dentist. She love her friend and caring person. She motivate herself. She hobbies drawing and listening to the music.

DEAR SISY'S

'LUV U'. First I want to say thanks for god for giving two pretty sisters for fighting, laughing,to love and take care of me. They're my world, soul and everything. I care of you even if I won't show this everytime around. I know that you guys love me too more than anyone else in the world. My love for you is endless..... You both gives me everything but sometimes I didn't give for you. We shared our clothes, foods, feeling, emotions and love eachother. Although I never really enjoyed sharing my things with you. We have always enjoyed sharing our childhood and love for each other. You both are most precious to me always. I cherish all our sweet and exciting childhood memories. No word can explain the love and affection you both have give me in my childhood and until now. My life would be dull and boring if God would not bless me with a sisters like you. In my point of view, there is no friend than a sister. Yes we always fight for chilly reason and tease and played with each other with unconditional love.

Sisters   Just a word with the emotions undefined

A synonym for MOM in our lives.

Yours lovingly,

Gowthami J

JANANI J

Janani Jayapal was born and raised in Chennai,Tamilnadu. She is a typical. Tradition South Indian girl who has a patriarchal family background. She is currently pursuing Masters in Business Administration at St. Joseph's college of engineering. She is a blogger who has written blogs to a caretaker company. She loves doing hand embroidery, music and hanging our with family and friends.

Instagram ID: candy_jaanuu

MY DEAR LOVELY VAISHU (VAISHNI V)

Friends are the important part of everyone's life. A friend is someone with whom you can share your joys and sorrows and who is there to help in case of need. I have lots of friends in school and college days. All are my good friends. Amongst them, Vaishni is a close heart friend who is very special to me. I am lucky enough to have true friend like vaishni. I value her friendship. Vaishni has many good qualities. Her helpful nature makes people to like here. My mother too fond of her. She is soft spoken and gives respect to elders.

She is an ideal girl and her behaviour is model for other students. Vaishni is very polite, good mannered and sweet tempered. She has a very cheerful nature. She is always helpful to others in their time of need and never feels them to be obliged. Due to her charming and winsome personality, she is liked by all. She takes active part in the college activities and encourage me take part. She motivates me to do well in studies and college activities. I am proud of my best friend vaishni. She is the source of joy and inspiration to me and all. She is a medicine to my life. It is a blessing to have a friend like vaishni and I am glad that I am getting lots of opportunity to learn many things from her. I would cherish her friendship forever and wish to keep her as my best friend forever. I can't imagine in my life without her.

LOVE YOU FOREVER.

Yours lovely bestiee,

Jaan…(JANANI J)

SUVEETHA J

Suveetha Jayapal born in Chennai, currently pursuing B.sci (computer science). She likes to wear traditional clothes. She love a lot here family and especially here both sisters. She hobbies watching tv, drawing and dancing

MY TINYY WORLD

I happy to say my tiny world is my family.
In my family we are 5 members. Mommy, Daddy & 2 sweet sisters. I am second daughter for my parents. There is lot of happy, love & care between us. Especially mommy is take care of our family beautifully. Mommy is bold character & straight forward person. She is mine inspired women. she always say us to stand in your own leg and achieve something in life. Next my hero daddy. He is genuine person .My daddy always had one special place in my heart. He give a lot of freedom to us. Daddy is my real hero. Next is mine sister janu .My sister teach me alot . One person who knows all about me is my 1st sister janu . I like here silent type character. Next is my fighter mine younger sister gowthami. She makes me energetic always . Among us alot of fights is gone but suddenly one small smile we joined within minute. Thus, about my tiny world. The only one place gave alot love for me is mine tiny world. I hope u have spent nice time with my tiny world. My family provided me with the proper information and inspiration for me to overcome the challenge of blindness.
Yours Lovely,
Suvee sweet (SUVEETHA.J)

SANTHOSH PANDIAN A

Santhosh Pandian A is from Chennai. He is pursuing an MBA Final year at St. Joseph's College of engineering. He is good at all the technical works in his department. He has been called Mr.Tech by his Professors. He is one who loves to do more volunteering work. He is passionate about helping people who need help to survive or for Education.

Instagram ID: santhosh__pandian

AN ILLUSIONARY DESIRES

Dreams are so many for a day, a week, a year, or a Lifetime. But all the dreams do not succeed, sometimes it may be bust by someone or it's busted like an illusion. An 11 years old boy, had a lot of desires. His first desire is to join the basketball team of his school, he joined and played well in it. Days passed away one day he wants around Rs.500 to buy a jersey for a zonal match. At this time his family has paid home rent of Rs.900. He asked for 55 percent of that, so he didn't get it. He asked his relatives and neighbours for money; they denied at the quoting "do study only, no games". There is no other way to go for him, he never wants to disturb his parents. It's the First illusion busted for him but he never wants to leave his co-curricular activities, He has been interested in some kind of volunteering so he joined scouts in his School. Here the problem arises again in the form of money, he needs a uniform for his Scout Camp. But this time he doesn't ask his father or mother, he decides himself. Yeah, the boy desires were busted like an ILLUSION. We came across many inspirational stories, most of the successful people who once struggled for money. But they get someone's help by their diligence. Here the boy gives up his desires for his family by understanding his family's financial situation. Here I am not saying that he doesn't have diligence because his world is too small so he showed his diligence to the fullest. At last, my Conclusion, we are in a world with a lot of happiness but we forget to find it out. Yeah, find your happiness by helping your loved ones, neighbours, or whoever needs help that should be grateful. LOVE TO HELP, HELPER GETS LOVE.

SIRUSHTIKA R S

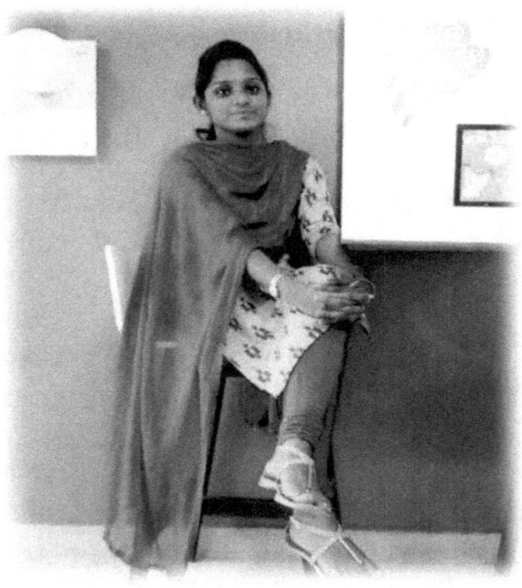

Sirushtika is from Chennai. She is pursuing MBA in final year at St. Joseph's College of engineering. She is good at her studies as well as extra-curricular activities and she was also a throw ball player at the district level. She is good in doing wall decors and handcrafts. She is a person who always spread positive vibes in her surroundings and has a helping tendency. She s a little bird that is chasing the dream.

Instagram ID: _sirushtika_rs

THE DREAM COMES TRUE

Everyone in this world has dreamt about something that they want in their life to happen, maybe a job, love, passion, and more. This story is about two birds who chased their dream and won the hearts of many people. This story was started at the school days, years passed and they both completed their schooling successfully and stepped towards college. Ankita and Kathir joined separate colleges and they meet daily evening and go home together. Kathir used to drop Ankita a few streets before Ankita's house. Kathir and Ankita had a wonderful bonding where they both never misunderstood each other. Kathir took Ankita to movies, beach, restaurants, parks, etc., and at the same time both concentrated on their studies too. Both studied well and scored good percentages. One day when Kathir and Ankita were on their way home at that time Ankita's uncle got them red-handed and taken both homes. They both were under pressure and it burst into a big problem and Kathir and Ankita were forced to come out of their relationship. One-week later Ankita's family took her to Hyderabad so that Ankita would forget about her love. Kathir started his career in a good company and was earning better. Though they were forced to separate they didn't give up. Both Kathir and Ankita were hiding their feelings for each other and stayed happily outside. After 2 years Ankita returned to Chennai with the same love and hope. Ankita started talking to Kathir on a landline when there is no one in the house and it went on. One day Ankita's family decided to see an alliance for her but Ankita refused and stood strong on her decision. On the other side, Kathir was in a good position and he also started saving money for his marriage without knowing his family. Ankita's family forced her to get married because of some neighbours who kept on urging Ankita's mother because of her age but Ankita always stood strong in her decision with hope and faith in God. After few years Ankita's family

accepted her love as she was stubborn, then they called Kathir and discussed the wedding and other formalities that have to be done but Kathir's family has no interest in this marriage and Kathir's mom told him that she won't be attending any functions and if you want to get married you can go out please don't come here. Ankita was upset and was not sure what to do. Ankita's family talked to Kathir's mother but she refused. Ankita and Kathir decided to get married with the support of Ankita's Family. Everyone got excited about their marriage and started shopping for the function. Kathir took Ankita's family and bought a Mangalya chain and marriage saree with his own savings. One fine day Kathir tied three knots with Ankita and now they have a girl child. Ankita and Kathir are having a blessed life with God's protection and family blessings. This is the story of the Dream comes true of Ankita and Kathir.

SWATHI NANDAKUMAR

Swathi is currently doing her 2nd UG in Guru Nanak College. She is an optimistic person. Swathi is passionated about Photography, Table tennis. She is a bibliophile, a foodie and a naturalist. She is a moody writer. She is an extremely friendly person and open type. She wants to fulfil her dad's wish of buying a home and wants to earn well for her family.

Instagram ID: bigmouth_foodie

HEALING YOURSELF

Being a normal person, you will go through stages of life like rejections, failure, depression, major setbacks, enemies, heartaches and more, Because that's life. Rising and coming back is important and powerful just like failing and learning a lesson. People might say 'move on', like nothing happened, but the tears are real and the pain is unbearable. You pour your heart out. Tears come non-stop. when you go through the worst phase, not giving up is important, you are alone and you learn a lot without others teaching you. Lot happens around you at the same time, It can be a family problem or financial problem or a breakup or betrayal or stress from workplace or having worries or a big loss like close one's death. Anything of the above can break you inside and make you so depressed and give you anxiety and insecurities. you learn and change the way you are; Accept the changes and challenges, grow through what you go through!

Give your body the time, your mind the space it needs. By allowing yourself to take the time and sort out, half things won't even matter to you. forgiving yourself is very necessary. By moving on, learning new things, your mind gets into a different path. go out, grab some coffee or go travel solo. Time will pass, your perspective will changer, Be care-free and do good, you will get great returns. Inner peace is important. Face your own challenges by overcoming the odds, the struggles, emotions and being scared of others opinion. Never give up. Take rest but never quit. Take a time out, sort things out in your head. Put yourself first because you matter. Be silent and observe, as maturity comes by experience and not by age.

Finally, by loving yourself, respecting yourself, by understanding what truly matters and being that little kid at heart, you will Rise Above Hate!

You HEAL YOURSELF on the whole process, because no one else will do it for you.

VASHCINI JS

Vashcini is a charming girl. She has the ability to write quotes and stories. She is a good listener. She involves in all activities with her own interest.
Instagram ID: Vashcini_js

INTERNET- THE VIRTUAL WAY OF LIFE

Introduction:
In today's world we find ourselves communicating more and more through online channels such as messaging, social media and video calls, often at the expense of face to face dialogue. There are certain situations where online communication is unavoidable but others where for virtual over real life conversations.

It is now easier than ever to access the internet, whether you are using a computer, phone or tablet. There is no doubt that many young people are spending more and more time online, with both positive and negative consequences.

Mobile phones have had an enormous impact on many aspects of our lives. They have significantly changed the way we communicate with each other in both our personal and our professional lives and they clearly have many advantages. However, there are several drawbacks.

Remember the benefits of internet :
Advantage of the internet is that young people can do research for their school work and homework. This often helps teenagers to widen their knowledge and improve their grades. Another positive aspect of the internet is that people can speak foreign languages by chatting to friends in other countries.

The most powerful argument in favour of mobile phones is that they can be used to call for help in the most inaccessible places. For example, when a car breaks down in a remote area and emergency services can be called to the scene of an accident without delay.

Negative consequences :
Some young people become addicted to online gaming and this can mean that they waste too much time playing these games . This can have a negative effect on their school work, the amount of exercise they got and their social lives. The most common criticism of mobile phones is the fact that we are now

expected to be available 24-7. A final negative effect is that in public places such as on trains or at the cinema, there is no escape from the noise of annoying ringtones and loud noises. Some experts are concerned that a lack of face to face interaction impedes the development of vital social skills such as emphasising and reacting to situations in real time.

To sum up:

Personally, I think the internet is an incredible tool and I believe that online communication brings an overall advantage in today's fast paced, global society.

K DHIVYA

K Dhivya is doing her final year MBA, and she is from Chennai, she was born and brought up in Chennai, her hobbies are cooking, listening to songs and watching movies.

SELF-LOVE

To Myself,
In this beautiful journey of life with me,
With baby steps to a grown up women,
It's just normal to everyone but only I know my journey,
Like waves in the sea it has highs and lows,
It's a cluster of happiness and sadness,
Everyone has a story I too have a story,
I may be a normal girl to everyone but I am the heroine of my story,
I am the queen of my palace,
With full of dreams and hope to reach the star, which is shining far away in the sky,
Trying to reach the golden star which twinkles at me in the dark sky.
Self-love,

SAMYUKTHA S

Samyuktha S born in Chennai, currently studying 12 th STD (biology group). Sam passion to become a cardiologist. She always have positive vibes . She love her family very much. Sam hobbies gardening, cooking and listening to music..

DEAR ROSHAN

Dear Roshan,

Love you dear, first thank you god. Because, you gave me a beautiful person in life .Without you I feel that my life is incomplete some places and incidents remained me about you. I know that you are not near to me but, always close to my heart. You are the person whom I can share my feelings and emotions. In my childhood, I lost my sister. But, you entered my life. You and fulfilled my wishes and her space in my life .You is my cutie pie. Whenever in a sad situation is used to remembered his face my lips automatically smiles. I have written a personal diary for you about all the incidents happened in my life when you are not with me but hopes and love. I will love him endlessly. God taught me that "life doesn't needs 100 of fake people it needs a one lovely person". I will wait for you till the end of my life, until you come. So, I am proud of writing this letter on your birthday Dec-13.

True friends are those who care without hesitation, remember without limitation, forgive without any explanation and love even with little communication. An empty stomach needs food, an empty brain needs knowledge, an empty house needs a family, and an empty heart needs love. But then, an empty life needs a friend, thanks for filling in.

Once again, love you Roshan
With lots of love,
Samyuktha

SASIKALA V

Sasikala is doing CSE in St. Joseph's College of Engineering. Where she is very much interested in coding. She is very much interesting in teaching. Now she is working as a teacher in tuition centre. She loves to play keyboard. Her hobby is to read devotional books..

Instagram ID: sasi_hema22

ROBBERY LINE UP

Once upon a time there lived four friends. One of them was a policeman, a bank officer, a hacker and the other one was just a normal person. They were planning to steal money from the bank officer's bank. The bank officer gives information about his bank daily to his friends. They follow the instructions and steal little by little. One day the bank management informed this to police and filed a complaint. The police officer who is taking charge is one of the partners in crime . So he accused someone and closed the case. One day the bank management planned to transfer a lorry full of money to their ATM's in the night at 12:30 am. The bank officer got this official information and then pass this to his friends and asked them to come immediately. Then he informed every moment going in via Bluetooth. The money refunders didn't set the alarm on that day. Then the robbers came there. And the hacker hacks all the cameras. Then they fill the entire bank with chloroform. Then all the bank officials fainted and fell down. Then the robbers stole the entire money from the lorry and bank and escape from that place. Next day morning this news wide-spread and this case handed over to the CID. Then the CID officer started his investigation. First he doubted the bank workers because without the workers this wouldn't be possible. Then he investigate the bank officer(the robber). The bank officer did not answer properly so he doubted him. After the investigation, the bank officer called his friends and told them everything. Then he asked his friend's to distort and take their individual shares. Then all of them were distorted and settled in various places. One of the robbers (the policeman) invested his money in real estate and planned to put the rest in savings. He is gonna deposit his savings in the new bank. A news flash on tv " a big amount is robbed from the other country bank" in the bank. While the robber deposits his money to the bank officer he notices the news and collects the

money and is shocked by seeing a bank seal in the money bundle. This a special seal which is used by the bank officials only. He doubted the depositor. Then he called and informed this issue to the other country's police officer. Then they came and arrested the robbers. Other three robbers were also arrested. They agreed about their robbery. They handed the leftover robbed amount to the police officer.

MORAL: Pennies make pounds

J MONESHASREE

Moneshasree is from Chennai, currently doing her third year in MBA integrated at St. Josephs college of engineering. She is good at her studies. She is a kind of girl who puts her maximum effort in everything she does. She is excellent in pencil sketching and also a wonderful nature admirer. She is a girl who always makes others feel comfortable. She is a good classical dancer and a girl who strives hard to taste success.

RÊVER

Dreams are not those which comes while we are sleeping, but dreams are those when you don't sleep before fulfilling them
-A.P.J. Abdul Kalam

Dream is something which is to be achieved, this dream differs from person to person based on their experience, imagination, thoughts etc. Each and every person in this universe can have dream. Dream maybe anything having a own house, to go and visit places, to taste any dishes etc. We can even have some higher dreams like to become an engineer, doctor or IPS officer etc. In young age children keep on changing their dream they won't be stable, because these are the dreams that they get by watching tv channels, because children watch many cartoon episodes and imagine that particular character as themselves and say I am going to become like this or that, But at a particular stage they come to understand everything, they try to identity their interest and start focusing on their interest so that they can develop their interest. That interest which they have on anything can be chosen as their dream. Having a dream alone is not enough, we must start working harder to achieve our dream. We can sacrifice anything for our dream, but we must not sacrifice our dream for anything. We must develop the courage to face problems that come to stop our dream. We must face the problems and not fear for the problem. It is not mandatory that we must have only one dream, we can have multiple dreams. But we must not think about all the dreams at a time and make it complicated, must achieve one by one. We must frame various steps to achieve the dreams. If the dreams cannot be achieved in a single attempt, we must go for second attempt, but in the second attempt we must identity the mistake made before and try to rectify those mistakes, these also play an important role for achieving the dream. The happiness that we get while achieving the dream and the result we receive for our hard work is always priceless. So to taste success the medicine named sacrifice and hard work is necessary.

A P RABHINA ROY

Through this piece of text our author A. P. Rabhina Roy despite her young age has taken her time to write this marvellous text. Like the saying "Roses do not bloom hurriedly" ,our writer has taken her time to give us this masterpiece.

Instagram ID: __.rabhi.__

MY INDIA MY PRIDE

My country , India has several names it goes with Hindustan and Bharat. It is a democratic country since the year 1950.After our independence from the British our former leaders have done their best to make our country better in every way. One thing that captivates everyone around the world is the fact we can find people of all religion and races here. Tourism ,food name it and we have it here. The famous saying

"Unity in diversity " makes India symbolize togetherness and harmony! We get through struggles and hardship together !You can see that through the IPL games. All of us expect the perfect holiday to be in a fancy resort in the states but we hold the strength here with innumerable temples, the serenity in the countryside !The game of minds ,Chess was invented in India .
This country has one of the most diverse cultures and variety ,However if it were to me ,I would like to change several things. In the old days to maintain peace different classes for people were introduced. Sooner or later it led to people being treated unfairly. The upper class always dominated and the lower classes were buried, Because of this even the gems in a sack of stones are lost !In a country where every human is given the same treatment irrespective of their class or caste is what we all live for. Child labour is one trait that brings India down,

I would prefer if every child in our land is given the capability to find and pursue their life goals and make a better future for them. In the year of 1986 a big step was taken through the child labour act. Every cloud has a silver lining , I hope in the future the false beliefs ,irrational caste system, child labour is all abolished and a better country with all the basic necessities for every single Indian is born!

A K PRATIBHA

A. K. Pratibha ,a passionate student has given her best to explicitly make us understand a snippet of the struggles in life.

CAN MONEY BUY HAPPINESS?

"Money is means, Not the end", This proverb accurately explains the balance of wealth and health in one 's life.
Ever since childhood we are taught that money solves everything ,But is it actually true? Is money more important than the relationships, peacefulness that one has? No, We must value every aspect of our life that has made us the person we are. If we let the greed in us to earn more and more guide us ,it will be like chasing a train while walking. We will lose in life. In the recent years, in India most youngsters hope they could get a job in the states. Because they are blinded by the greed for money they leave, they become distant with their own parents and family. Even in emergency situations it is mostly impossible for them to help their family. A lot of money will also put a stop to the creativity and produce a negative effect on children.
However ,do we need money to sustain life? Yes !
"Money talks". If you are rich and wealthy you are given the utmost care in this judgemental world.

 All of us gain happiness from serving others, By serving I mean helping and making them happier. Doing these acts have proven to makes us feel elated and proud of ourselves. Sharing our wealth is what makes our lives worth living. The main reason one needs money is to buy whatever he or she desires. It also makes the person feel better when they don't have to worry about financial problems when they wake up.
My opinion is that we all need money for leading a life which is a little less stressful. So let us all keep in mind to never let our greed make the better of us and lead a better and meaningful life.

VASANTH N

Vasanth is from Chennai. He is a Commerce Graduate, current pursuing MBA at St. Joseph's College of Engineering. He is interested to play music instruments like piano, drums and mridangam. He is an extrovert and doesn't care about people's thoughts on him. He is lovable and caring in nature. He loves to learn new things daily and keeps on updating himself.
Instagram ID: itz_sharath.0978

AN EVERLASTING RELATIONSHIP

There are many types of relationships in our life and in this world. A relationship is easy to create but it is so hard to make it stronger and lasting. A long lasting relationship is very easy to establish if we put the spirit of trust and love in our hearts. Logically, A strong relationship gives birth to an enjoyable living. The two main characters for a good relationship are "LOVE AND TRUST".

"LOVE ALL, TRUST A FEW, DO WRONG TO NONE" (William Shakespeare)

Firstly LOVE, is the greatest gift in the whole world. We cannot define Love in specific. But we the people misinterpret Love with possessiveness and jealousy. But Love is all about that one person to share the blessings with someone whom the person choose to spend his/her life time with. When we love someone from the bottom of out heart we give everything of ourself instead of asking. We communicate and we create a bond with our partner and as a result we become one instead of two.

"LOVE IS AN INVISIBLE THREAD THAT TIES TWO HEARTS TOGETHER"
Secondly TRUST, which is the second requirement of a lasting relationship. Trust is broken once is broken forever. Sometimes we think that trust can be picked up again but it is not true. When we lose trust from someone we cannot gain trust about them easily. Trust should be maintained by each side of a relationship. Rebuilding trust is the hardest work in life. It can be compared with a glass. When a glass is broken, it's pieces can be picked up and can be joined again but the perfect glass can never be made because the sign of broken pieces will alive. Losing trust is the first step of losing love.

Because when we love someone we give respect to them, we let them enjoy their freedom, let them enjoy their life, we give them everything and for exchange we would want them to respect our feelings and trust that we have on them.

"TO BE TRUSTED IS A GREATER COMPLIMENT THAN BEING LOVED"

We should create such relationship where the freedom and happiness will exist. So we must give importance to love and trust in our relationship and life.

RAMYA PRABHAKARAN

Ramya Prabhakaran is a final year student at St. Josephs College of Engineering and currently taking up a master's degree in Business Administration. As a Business student she aspires to start her dream business. She is a person filled with positive energy and thoughts. She is a well-rounded individual who lives with passion, dedication and grace.

Instagram ID: r_a_m_y_a__prabhakaran

GRAVITY OF POSITIVITY

All of us wonder about how to become successful in life. Sometimes we find ourselves running towards our goals to shape our future but there are times when we might not be able to navigate our way to success. That is the time when we need positive thoughts, the most in our lives. Positive thinking is the only way to overcome hardships. Positive thinking combined with positive actions will eventually result in success.

If your mind is clear, free of worries, you can stay more focused and concentrate better on your goals. When you have positive thoughts in your mind, it clears away a lot of worries and distraction from us. This way we get more energy to focus and work for what we really aspire to achieve. Maintaining positive thinking helps our brain become positive as well and work that way.

We became what we think. If we fill up our brain with positive thoughts it will fire up that way. It works in the opposite way as well. If your brain is filled with negative thoughts, it's highly like that they may turn out to be true. The more energy you have the more you can invest it to be successful in life. Positive thoughts not only give us positive energy, but also decrease the negative energy by keeping all the worries and distractions at bay. Positive vibes and positive environment are important for mental peace and growth of all individuals in the world.

Having known how important positivity and positive thoughts are to stay on our way to success, it is equally important to know how we can maintain positivity around us, upkeep our positive thoughts and most importantly fight the negativity around and inside us. There will always be some negativity around you be it some negative people, be it a song, movie, place, anything makes you feel negative, do not give a second thought before eliminating it from your life.

Last but not least, overthinking brings the maximum negativity. Don't overthink scenarios in your head. Do not worry a lot about your future and results. If you can really do something about what is bothering you, take immediate action if not, forget about it and do what you really can. Do not fear failures; do not let them come in way of even your slightest chance to be successful.
Think Positive, do positive, be positive and then, hope for positive results.

RAJESHWARI ELANGO

Rajeshwari is pursuing her BA . English Literature in Shri shankaral sundharbai shasun Jain college . In this writing she kept her poin towards women empowerment to show how well a women has got a position to show up her self in society .
Instagram ID: miss_fairy_queen

EMPOWER WOMEN EMPOWERED WOMEN

Women are educating much better than men's in present generation. We can see women employees in various fields as a result of women empowerment. Let me raise a question so that you could get a proper retort. Do you think that all women are left to do what they desire? I probably think that you will get a clear respond. When a woman is sent to pursue her higher studies she is not allowed to choose what she wishes to, instead she is fixed to study a particular thing which she is offered by her own surrounding. When she overlap her job she is said as a mannerless fellow somewhere just because of the job she choose as her career. In our country nearly 54% parents allow their kids to do what they want, then what about the other 46% families. They are afraid of their society instead of thinking what their kids desire. In some families reputation is important than someone's ambition. Families need to understand that a girl kid is there in a safe environment unless or until we teach our boy kids how to see and respect a women in his same society. When a women is praised as God, then why can't a women do what she desires to? As a God a women is good enough in taking decisions in other's lives but as a mortal body she is pushed down stating that her desire would take her in a problematic way so, she is said to do something, and she is also pushed forcefully to do something. Some where she kills herself just because everyone keeps a barrier in her dreams and goals. Women's are empowered but not in the way they wanted to be empowered.

SHARON HRITHIKA S

Sharon Hrithika is a mallu girl who is born in Kerala, brought up in Chennai. Who has a descent accent in English and Tamil but a funny one in Malayalam. She is a management student who is currently pursuing MBA. She is also a blogger and has contributed to a caretaker company. Sharon has great passion for photography and she considers faith and family to be the most important to her.

Instagram ID: sharonhrithika

A SIMPLE SMILE

A simple smile can change someone's day, yes I'm talking about a real smile, a heartwarming smile, a smile that comes from within. A smile is an effortless action that speacks louder than words.it says,
"I like you
You make me happy
I am glad to see you"

Research has shown that smiling make your brain release serotonin and dopamine-neurotransmitters that produces feelings of happiness and wellbeing.

The effect of a smile is powerful even if it is unseen. Telephone companies throughout the United States have a programme called "Phone Power". In this programme they suggest the employees to smile while talking on the phone cause your smile comes through, in your voice.

Each and every person in the world seeking happiness and there is one simple way to find it. That is by controlling your thought. Happiness depends on one's inner conditions.

Smile at the world and the world will smile back to you. Make a difference in other lives... simply by smiling!

SHAKINA M P

Shakina M P, a product of the 90's. She is graduated from Anna University, and now pursing her management studies. She is a voracious reader and loves pen down her thoughts. She loves to add a unique and creative touch in everything she does. She is passionate about travel, gardening and arts. She reads a lot of world politics and history kinda stuffs. She finds solace in cooking anything incorporated with cheese. She is an unfettered soul, picks random interests and hobbies to seize her day.

# TO BE OR NOT TO BE: THAT IS THE QUESTION

We have spent almost a year indoors, due to the outbreak of covid-19. People have started to adopt and live with the new normal life during this unprecedented time.

I wonder whether this has happened in history before. The world is being shut down, things have become still, yet we call it a war against an unknown enemy. If only we know the unknowns of the known. We can live in the menace of the distant war, seeing the increasing rate of morbidity and mortality or accepting things and evolve for the new world. This new foe has brought us together virtually. We live more on the digital platform rather than the real world. Perhaps, it's the situation that has inclined us digitally.

This lockdown is indeed a dream holiday I have been wishing for, to take a break from regular classes and exams. It was a pleasure to wake up late, attend classes in bed with snacks to munch and parents to pamper. There was plenty of time to watch my favorite series, read books, pick up new hobbies, and spend time with family and pets. It was a really long nice holiday. Sometimes, I do feel bored and desperately wished to resume life before the covid-19 crisis. Now, the vaccine is discovered, what can we expect from 2021? How long will it take, for the Marshall plan to be executed? How will the vaccine reach everyone, in this rudderless global leadership and economies? LOL, that was quite a bit too much.

The world is rapidly evolving and changing every day. Every time there has been a change, and innovation there blooms a new realm of opportunities for those who see it. It might not be the same world that had been a year ago that we used to live in. The new horizon is waiting for us to step in.

Let's do little things that make us happy until then. Stay away from social media. Rearrange your living room. Explore that untouched loft that holds loads of your childhood and distant

memories. Listen to your loved ones. Ping that old school friend whom you haven't been in contact for a long time. Write down your wildest unimaginable dreams without any stinginess. If you can read this, you sure do have access to a university of colossal language. Learn that language you have fancied for. The list never ends, find your heart, and follow wherever it takes you (within your home, obviously).

The things will get better, the spread will be curbed, have faith; covid-19 shall too pass. Soon the red shall change to orange and the orange to green and we shall resume.

JAYASHREE S

Jayashree is pursuing 2nd year of B.E - Geo Informatics in CEG, Anna University Chennai. Her native is Arani.
Instagram ID: jayashree 9996

NO GOOD MOVIE IS TOO LONG AND NO BAD MOVIE IS SHORT ENOUGH

Every great film should seem new every time you see it - Art is the closest we come to understanding how a stronger really feels personally I don't watch film for money if I go to the theatre to watch films, after seeing film I become a new person Every time. In my point of view cinema has been a part of my life from my birth. It had created a massive impact on my life and cinema has helped me to overcome.my lows in my tough situation.as cinema has evolved greatly in recent years cinema for me personally is a great escape from real life and helps us gaining knowledge about how different people lead their lives.

CINEMA - "A RECREATION"

Since the inception of the existence of man has been discovering different ways for recreation and cinema is one such discovery. Cinema is the dominating recreation meant for relaxation. earlier days of relaxation were experienced with limited restriction, but as we evolved cinema has changed the way of life, cinema has influenced many people personally myself and has impacted me in many ways. Cinema is a break for people's take from a long , stressful hours of their everyday lives. In my point of view cinema surface the reality and tell us the truth but we often find it hard to accept.

BABITHASHREE S

Babitha is a kind of funny, friendly, optimistic, sensitive person. She likes to draw people like capturing their happy moments. She is wish to serve her country and uplift it.

Instagram ID: night_fury_124

RAPID GROWING TECHNOLOGY

Have we ever noticed how much the technology around us has changed compared to our school life and our college life? Think about our parents' college life. In those days they used to wait for a phone call and rush to booths but these days we used to put our flooded phones in mute. Do you realize how many of us are keeping our ring volume full at least? Even our way of thinking is different from our parents'. What is the reason behind these? One of the main reasons according to me is this easily accessible technology.

Humans are becoming slaves of their own inventions. Many of us really don't even realize how much this technology around us has taken up our life. It's good to have help for our work but it should not make us incapable of doing that work in the future. For example, calculators, this thing is very useful but nowadays we are using it for many small additions like calculations too which is very much sad to say.

It's good to have technological growth but it should not ruin ourselves. I am not blaming the scientists who have invented those, I am talking about us the users. We should develop a clear idea in our mind first. If I start talking about smartphones this article won't end. We heard many speaking about the use of smartphones. I wish to convey that it's more fun to talk to people through call or in person than chatting. I think this exact thing is lagging in the current generation, communication. I am speaking of this as I too had this issue. If you too have the same don't worry just grow a habit of calling and speaking to person and improve your communication skills. Happy talking:)

BERTINA S

She is 19 years old and loves reading novels. Her hobbies include listening to and composing music. She is hardworking and quick to learn things quickly.

HUMILITY

"True humility is not thinking less of yourself, it is thinking of yourself less."
- CS Lewis.
In this preoccupied world where man is so focused on chasing after the insignificant and empty things of the world, it is very easy to forget the things that actually matter.
We are so swayed away by greed, pride, lust and are so self centered that we rarely ever think of anything other than us, other times we spend all our time and energy into things that the world expects from us even if it's not something that we actually want to do.
In the end what matters is not how much money you've saved up or how many followers you've got on social media. What matters is what you leave behind on this planet.
Now, all of us can't be Steve Jobs or Mother Theresa's but we can impact and brighten the lives of the people around us.
Check in with the neighbour who lives alone, call the friend you've been meaning to call, help out at home, the list goes on. When I was in my 2nd semester of college, they took us to an orphanage, I remember seeing the kids there, they were all so excited to see us. They performed a skit, sang a few songs, I'd never forget this one action song they sang, "If your happy and you know it clap your hands" they were all smiling and singing it but the happiness didn't reach their eyes, it was almost as if it was forced. I realised how blessed I was to have my parents and so many other people that care deeply about me. That day at the orphanage, my friends and I got all the birthdays of the little kids there and we do a little celebration on their birthdays. This might not seem like much for us but you brighten up their day, the day they think so much about, they're so confused and riddled with questions like what is their purpose here? why are they here in a place like this? and so many other questions. It's not fair for them and you may not have the power to change

their past but your presence there brightens up their day gives them a little bit of hope and encourages them to live and gives them courage to move on.

Helping one person might not change the world, but it will change the world for that person.

I believe that is our purpose here, being a ray of sunlight in this abyss of darkness we call home.

Humble yourselves in the sight of the Lord and He shall lift you up. (James 4:10.)

SUBIKSA V

Subiksa V is a student of College of Engineering Guindy, Anna University pursuing B.E. Geo Informatics II nd year. She is an optimistic and a broad minded person. She is a determined girl. Patience is her main companion. She is an outgoing person and funny with people. She is hugely devoted to her works. Her great interest and involvement in writing made her ink this article. She had achieved her goal of making people know the importance of stress free life. This budding writer is in her way to great success.

Instagram ID: sweeet_n_spicyy

WAVES OF LIFE

Few days ago, I've gone to a beach, walking alone on the seashore, feeling the blowing ocean breeze and the cool water touching the toes. The beauty of Mother Nature mesmerized me. I felt relaxed, just soaked up the environment around me. I was out of the world, many thoughts started wandering inside me. I felt something unusual at that moment. I stared at the waves and stood still for some time. Something disturbed my mind. When I heard the crash of the waves, I felt that the sea was trying to communicate with me. As time passed, I began to understand that the journey of waves and the journey of life were very relatable.

"Life is like a wave which has many rises and falls but finally reaches the shore. Even though there are ups and downs, one day you will reach greater heights in life. Let the dirt of sorrow be pushed off from the sea of happiness. Discover the unique pearls in you which are invaluable. As the wave curls itself to rise higher, shape your body and mind to achieve bigger. Let your restless soul become free as the tides reach the shore. Enjoy the splash of water on face. Be a surfer who can overcome all the tides of challenges and travel till the end, not a surfer who will drown in the sea of failures. No matter how hard the storms are, just sail your boat against the wind to survive in life."

Hours passed and I realized that some life lessons are learnt only through patience. The sound of waves taught me what life was. As the sunlight patted my wet clothes, they began to dry and I felt that the stress in my heart also evaporated and diffused into air…

POOJA

Pooja from Chennai, TamilNadu. She graduated from Vels University (BSC Computer Science) and currently pursuing her Post graduation (MBA [HR & Finance]) in St. Joseph's College of Engineering. Besides being a Department second topper she is interested in Sports. Being a State Level Throwball Player after achieving several trophies her hungry for achieving in sports has not stopped. It's been 11 years being in a sport and hungry for each trophy has never stopped. She wants to be a Independent Women who should be successful in Passion and Profession. She wants to be Great HR as of now and should move forward ahead and should write more Anthologies.

SPACE FOR WOMEN

In every field we see only Men everywhere as compared to Women. Once upon a Time my passion was to become a Astronaut. Only few people in Space Research are Women that lead me to dream and make as my passion. While we started talking about space the first which come to our mind was "Who was the first person who stepped on the moon?" Of course its Neil A Armstrong, the second person was Michael Collins and the third person was Edwin E Aldrin Jr.

The above three persons achieved and shown us we can land in Moon. After that 24 astronauts went to the Moon and 12 of them had the opportunity to walk on it. On July 20, 1969, Neil Armstrong became the first human to step on the moon. He and Aldrin walked around for three hours. From 1969 to 2020 none of the women astronauts had went to Moon. At last the first cadre of astronauts for NASA's Artemis program is made up of 18 people and nine of them are Women. Their names were announced at a December 8 National space council meeting at Kennedy space center in Florida. The Artemis program aims to return a human presence to the moon this decade.

Nine of the 18 selected astronauts are women. Among the astronauts today is one of the five NASA crew members currently and working in orbit. Kate Rubins was selected in the astronaut class of 2009 and arrived at the International Space Station in October for a six-month stint. The flight is her second, she also flew in 2016. During that mission, Rubins became the first scientist to sequence DNA in orbit.

The first and foremost Women who inspired us in Space Research Kalpana Chawla was an American astronaut, engineer and the first woman of Indian origin to go to space. She first flew on Space Shuttle Columbia in 1997 as a mission specialist and primary robotic arm operator. Kalpana Chawla is the first women from India became a Astronaut and went for

space shuttle. Her first mission was successful and the second mission made her space research to the end. The spacecraft to become unstable and break apart. After the disaster, space shuttle flight operations were suspended for more than two years, similar to the aftermath of the Challenger disaster.

On 5 February 2003, the prime minister of India announced that the meteorological series of satellites, MetSat was to be renamed "Kalpana". The first satellite of the series, "MetSat-1", launched by India on 12 September 2002 was renamed "Kalpana-1".

In this Modern world Women are achieving in all fields. Now the time began for the Moon Walk also. The equality that we needed was also going to establish in the Outer World also. These women's are one among the Inspiration for the younger generation to achieve something more then anyone else in the world.

VIDHYASRI K

Vidhyasri is from Chennai and she is currently pursuing MBA. She is simple and jovial character. She loves doodling and crafts.

Instagram ID: vidhyasrik16

ENJOY LITTLE THINGS

Happiness is little things happening in day-to-day life of everyone but in this busy world nobody is focusing on the little things which happening around them.

Waking up early just to see the sunrise in the beach wearing the favourite hoodie and the waves touching your legs….

When you are craving for snack and suddenly your mom makes you the aloo tikki and serves it with ketchup….

When you are waiting for the bus and the dog passes by wagging tails at you….

When you went for shopping and the baby in the store smiles at you….

When any elderly people bless you for all success in your life….

When your friends visit your home just to surprise you….

When you spend your own money to buy gifts for your parents….

When unknown person wishes you on your birthday….

When your favourite song plays in the radio….

Even more…

These are the little things which is happening in our day-to-day life but we are not cherishing it. So, start to enjoy the little things trust me you are going to love it. Focus on the little things which gives happiness because little things matter the most than the others. So, enjoy the little things and spread happiness around you.

NIVEDHA BALAMURUGAN

Nivedha Balamurugan is born in Salem and settled in Chennai. She is currently pursuing MBA from St. Joseph's college of engineering. She is a NCC cadet. She is a part-time sketching artist. She is passionate about sketching and painting. She loves to do craft works. She is interested to learn new art techniques. She loves public speaking. She is a blogger. She likes entertaining people with her jokes and makes people happy with her art works.

Instagram ID: pencilartz73

AVOCATION, I ADORE

The first word that comes into our mind when we hear someone asking or talking about hobbies is something enthusiastic and entertaining. The concept is that doing something that makes us happy. So whenever this question arises towards me, I always think of drawing, sketching, painting and so on. These are the words that keep me alive and to which I fall in love with. I forget myself and my time flies away whenever I enter into an art store! All artistic kinds of stuff are amazing, right? We have seen many food lovers, bike lovers, car lovers, etc. But I am proud to say that I am an "Art lover".

Let me begin with my art life journey. Being daughters of artistic parents, it is a genetic thing that I am always crazy about this. During my childhood, I didn't realize that I am going to be this much passionate about arts. But my interest increased day by day. Everything starts from nothing. According to this as a kid, I used to draw only stick figures to represent the humans like we all used to do. But I always wanted to improve my sketching skills.

The school days were beautiful times when we had drawing sessions as a part of our academics. My friends and teachers used to appreciate me for my skills. I remember the day when I secured a "C" grade in my drawing exam when I was a small kid. I drew a boy with a flying kite. I thought it was looking good that I will score a higher grade. But my results broke my heart. I found that many other friends scored better than me and their pictures were good. At that instant, I felt like I was cheating myself by thinking that I am a good artist. No one knew my feelings to encourage me.

After a few days, my mother showed me a small painting which was a hut on a farm and a man watering the trees. It was simple realistic that was made by my father. The man in the picture was the same thing that I was trying to draw all those

days. I was wondering how talented he was but never expressed it. After a few years, I was going through my mother's biology record notebook and I was thrilled after seeing it. Her handwriting, the clarity of the sketches, the way she had neatly maintained her notebook for all those years was awesome. That was a jaw-dropping moment for me. They are my inspirations.

Now I have improved a lot. I started making people happy with my commissioned sketches. I follow my mom's way of maintaining artworks neatly. I hope my parents are proud of me now.

MANJARI BALAMURUGAN

Manjari Balamurugan is born and settled in Chennai. She is currently pursuing a B. Tech Information technology from St. Joseph's College of Engineering. She is passionate about doing art and craft works. She is deeply interested in painting. She loves cats. She loves helping people. She is interested in singing and blogging. She gives a lot creative ideas in terms of small business developmental activities.

Instagram ID: _.manjari

THE VALUE OF LIFE

Life is so unpredictable no one is going to know what is going to happen next. Our journey of life begins in the very safest place, our mother's womb. It takes 38 weeks, a pretty long time to create us into a beautiful soul. We stepped into this world with a great struggle and sacrifice given by her. From there our life started, every second is a blessing and this life is a great gift from god. Each day is a new beginning. Everyone should have a goal. It may be a short-term or a long-term goal to keep your life in a better place. It's better to set a goal daily and complete it before going to bed. It will give you confidence that you are becoming a better person every single day without wasting time on unwanted things. Time is very important as everyone says yesterday is yesterday that cannot be got back again. Never regret what you did, just do it in a better way next time. No one knows where? when? our journey of life is going to end. Whenever a good or bad thing happens in our life, it happens for a reason. Never feel bad or feel down for your failure. Every failure teaches you a priceless lesson that cannot be obtained by money or anything else, it can be learned only by your experience. Whatever happens in your life, never think of ending your life. You don't have any rights to do it. No one is perfect in this world, everyone has some negative qualities in them. You can't go back and recreate yourself. The only thing you can do is make your negatives into positives. Things can be changed when your perspective of viewing matters are changed. Nothing is impossible, if there is a will, there's a way. If you are ought to do something or passionate to do it, work until you get it. Never leave your hope on it. Failures may come to make you into a better person. And another important thing to be happy is to never expect anything from others. Whenever your expectation breaks it will surely hurt you in some way. Try to control your emotions. Once you learned to control your emotions, you are

the boss in your world. No one comes with you till the end. You came alone to this world, you will go alone. At the end of everything, always remember that you are there for you. Do whatever makes you happy. Life can be lived once! Be happy always and spread happiness and positivity wherever you go.

SWETHA PILLAI

Swetha is an engineering graduate plus a software engineer currently who has passion for art and writing. She enjoys writing stories as much as she loves to paint. She is a very creative and energetic person who loves to try new things and challenge her potential.

Instagram ID: swetha_pillai_

ONLY HUMAN!

It is okay!

Life can be hard, you may not get to do what you really want but it doesn't mean you should stop. You will get your chance all you have to do is have a little patience and keep working for it, you will get there. Even if the things you want is delayed, never stop doing what you love. Life is too long to be doing the same thing every day again and again. Break the routine.. take a pause.. give things second chance.. have another approach. It is okay to make mistakes.. it is okay to fail, but never forget to do it again and do it better this time. Go with the flow you are not an expert to know everything right at the beginning, you can learn after all we are only human. It is okay! So don't stress yourself and take every moment you get to enjoy life. So take a few minutes to do simple things to make your heart smile.

Just 5 minutes okay!

Take 5 minutes a day to spend for yourself. It is little less right, but let it be. The first minute thing about what you want to do in the next 4 minutes that would lift up your mood or would make you really happy, like listening a song or dancing to it or doing a sketch may be reading a book, how about a small game, just choose that you love. So now that it is decided let's do it for the next 4 minutes, if you are enjoying that then continue doing it for as much as time you can spend for it. There are no terms and conditions here that it's only 5 minutes but my rule is at least 5 minutes a day.

Now that you have taken 5 minutes for yourself, try to steal another 5 minutes to spend it with your loved ones, your family or your friends, for the ones who are important to you. Because life is too long to spend it alone with computers and phone. After all we are only human..

PREETHI L

Preethi loganathan is from Chennai, currently doing her third year MBA Integrated at St. Joseph's college of engineering .she is good at digital marketing. She won national level kabbadi player .she is very intelligent in tackling the situation and also good at predicting the future while doing a work .she has a friendly moving girl with everyone she meets.

Instagram ID: Preethu_loganathan

LIFE IS FULL OF MIRACLE AND SUPRISES

Life is full of surprises and miracles from our young age to old age we don't know what we are going to do and even if we have plan we don't know whether it will happen according to our plan.

In these many years we have met so many people and some people have given you good memories and some people gave you the bad memories.

In our life circle if anything happened long before maybe 2 to 3 years, it will be considered as memories according to us these maybe good or bad memory, the way we think it matters.

But, one important thing every situation gives you a good lesson in your life. We must be brave enough to handle these critical situation. There are some people who always want to taste only success in their life and they never care about others.

There are some who will always be there for us in our good and bad times let it be our parents, friends or anyone. They do everything for us without any expectations. And those peoples are born treasures in our life.

If something which we was longing to happen for many years for example if you were longing to do higher studies in any foreign countries but you didn't get chance for many years suddenly your college professor gives you a surprise saying you got a chance for studying in foreign country that too in scholarship how will that moment be? you will be very excited and you be very happy and you feel surprised and you will be filled with happiness.

That is life we doesn't know what will happen the moment later. so get ready to face all the things in our life because life is all about surprises and miracles.

SURUDHI RAJASEKARAN

This is Surudhi Rajasekaran from Tamil Nadu, Currently pursuing Master's in Instrumentation. She is Calm, Humble and a Cheerful soul, who is concerned about doing social activities and loves to explores the World. She aspires to excel in every possible field. She wears the armour of optimism and self-confidence. She likes to express unconditional feelings into simple words.

Instagram ID: surudhi_98

THE NEW ENDING

"Everything starts beautifully, Everything", they say.
But let me tell you not everything starts beautifully. Some start like it's the end. Yes, you read that right. There are few relations in this whole damn universe which start like this. I won't mention but I'm pretty sure you'd understand.
Now tell me, Why do you always wander around searching for a beautiful soul?
Please don't give me reasons like, "we search for a beautiful heart, not for a beautiful soul". This is a whole damn lie. I have heard it N number of times. But the truth is, you search for beautiful souls and not for the beautiful hearts. Tell me, why do you always blame love when you suffer from a Heartbreak?
"Just because it broke us" you'd say.
Now what if I say you ditched love?
It's shocking, right?
But why? Why does only love get blamed every time? What is its fault? Love is just an EMOTION in your heart. That's it. Out of N number of emotions if one of them leaves, why do you even think that your heart is in pieces? Tell me?
Why do you think, "People do not change, their priorities change?"
You know what, People do change. In fact they change every second. Changing is a continuous process. It's not in your hand. Maybe, Options arrive and priorities change. But don't forget that "People do change".
Tell me, why do you consider forever is a myth?
If forever is a myth then sadly "Humanity too is a myth". Why do you blame forever, when it is the feeling that changes?
Sadly, we are contaminating our hearts with the emotions we don't need and are washing out love from the heart.
There's a purpose to life's events, to teach you how to laugh more or not to cry too hard. You can't make someone love you, all you can do is be someone who can be loved, and the rest is

up to the person to realize your worth. We spend too much time looking for the right person to love or finding fault with those we already love, when instead we should be perfecting the love we give. No one can go back and make a brand new start. Anyone can start from now and make a brand new ending. There isn't promise of days without pain, laughter without sorrow, sun without rain, but can promise strength for the day, comfort for the tears, and light for the way. A day will come when people will be thirsty for love.

Maybe, That would be THE END.

SRI VAISHNAVI P

Sri Vaishnavi was born in Salem and brought up in Chennai, currently pursuing M.B.A. with a specialization in HR & Finance. She is a kind-hearted, friendly, and honest person with a full of positive attitude. She is a fantasy lover and she loves to learn & explore new things and also does many social activities. Now she had penned down to write her thoughts, to spread positivity in her fantasy world.

NEVER GIVE UP

Have you ever felt like giving up, as things are not happening as you expected? Do you feel low, depressed, and overwhelmed with negative emotions because of the ups and downs that inevitably come in life? Do you feel like you want to quit?

Then do remind yourself that behind every successful person who attempted more than once to reach his or her goal, would have followed these four words Never, never give up. All of us have many dreams in our minds, but hardly a few will work hard and manage to get them fulfilled in the first attempt or will try again and again unless they achieve their desired dream. Dreaming is the sweetest thing ever in our life because we always dream and hopes it work, to achieve them and change them to reality and never giving up in any situation. But for most of persons, their dreams are just dreams forever. This is because many of us will try but will not try again and again until we reach our dream. At some point of time, we do feel that it will not work. At this time, the only thing that we should have in our mind is Never give up. "Never give up" means keep trying and never stop working for your goals. This is the only tonic of our life when we are facing a tough situation on the way to reach our dreams. When we were all small babies, at that time we learned to walk by trying and trying many times. We do fall but we never gave up. We kept on trying and when we made it, our face was filled with full of joy and happiness. This is how we were doing at our early ages but why not now?

Have it in mind "Winners never quit, and quitters never win". If you want to be a winner then, "Never give up". Be confident, bold, and never ever lose hope if you fail. Failure will make us learn from our mistakes which was a barrier to our success. Think that failure is an opportunity given to correct our mistakes and which will be our lessons from which we can

learn a lot to shape our life and our way towards achieving our dream. Try, try, try, and try again and again unit you climb the mountain don't step back and feed your mind with full of success and the lessons learned from your failure. And remember success is doing ordinary things extraordinary well. You have to risk going too far, to discover just how far you can really go to achieve your dream. The major value in life is not what you get. The major value in life is what you become. We must all suffer for one of the two things in our life which is the pain of discipline or the pain of regret and disappointment in achieving our dreams. But, we should keep in mind that when we know what we want, and want it bad enough, we will definitely find a way to get it. No matter how big hurdle arises we can come out of it. As a child of the god we are all gifted will all will power that we need to lead our life. So never ever worry about anything. Just keep repeating this phrase in your mind " If not me, who else can? Always remember that you can turn the impossible into the possible. " NEVER GIVE UP".

VINOTH M

Vinoth is a strong, hardworking NCC cadet pursuing his final year of Mechanical Engineering at CEG, Anna University. His special talents include drawing portraits, organizing things, etc.

Instagram ID: trichy_artist

INDIAN NAVY

Peace keeping white battalion
When war arrive fight like stallion
Sky above, sand below, peace within
It's the place where they guard
Who were considered next to God
They don't have any big expectation
Except to see India, a well-developed nation
Their visions are always high
As they fly the tri colour victoriously in sky
Once a Captain said his wife
"If I die, don't cry in white saree,
Salute in white uniform, instead"
Hats off! To those peace guardians out there
For protecting our tomorrow
By giving their today.

SRIRAM CHIDAMBARAM ILANGOVAN

Sriram was brought up in Chennai. He is a typical Chennaiite who likes to hang out with friends and goes to movies often. He is currently working in a software firm but wishes to become an entrepreneur, and so has plans to do an MBA in the future. Apart from that, he has a good sense of humor and loves to do Stand-up comedy.

Instagram ID: sriramchidambaram

BRIDGING THE GAP

Has there been any circumstance wherein you have gone to a new city for work (say job-related travel or on vacation) without having UBER or OLA installed on your smartphone? If yes, then I can indubitably say that it would have been your worst nightmare.

If you are around 20 years of age, you ought to have had a lot of night stay and should have been hungry around 3 am, or rather you would have eaten dinner at 3 am (ironical but true XD). The 3 am biriyani shops are a new trend. These are hotspots for the youths today.

Looking at the abstract title, the expectation from this essay would have been a philosophy where people talk about reaching eternal destiny or the purpose of life or knowing about who you are. But what these UBER and 3 am biriyani shops got to do with "Bridging the gap"? :p

This write-up deals with people minting money by bridging the gap in society.

Take the first scenario of UBER. There were times when we had to walk from the house to the main road and wait for a bus to come or eagerly wave our hands to auto-rickshaws hoping they were empty, but only in vain. We were ready to pay money but needed comfort and wanted to save time. On the other hand, there were auto and cab drivers who couldn't find their customers efficiently. This was a gap in society. And people didn't realize it, except for some. UBER sensed this and converted it to a business idea of connecting the drivers and travelers (in a simple context, they mapped the producers to consumers). That is all they did, and now their revenue is in crores.

Let us move to the 3 am biriyani shops. People realized that staying awake for a long time at night can make them hungry. All they did was, dug the refrigerator but only managed to get the half-full Appy fizz bottles. Few people sensed this gap and started their business venture with the mid-night food joints. Their revenue too scales in lakhs.

It is not only the monetary capital that is a prerequisite to a business. There are many more.

SHWETAA S H

Shwetaa (Age- 23) is born in Madurai and settled in Chennai, who is now working in an IT company after MBA. A Korean language lover, who has learnt to speak fluently. She is a Multi lingual, friendly person who loves to do Social voluntary activities and Do a variety of hobbies, like Drawing, dancing, singing, translating etc. She also likes to listen to songs, BTS. She is a Happy go person who likes to learn all time and is always curious.

Instagram ID: shwe_hyyh

FINDING ME - INSPIRED FROM BTS

I would like to start from where I started my journey. I was a very normal, quiet , shy student who doubted herself, Hesitated to even speak in front of 4 people, hesitated to even stand up for something, be it a competition or even voicing out my opinion. That's when i found BTS, in 2014 when i was in High school. I have been growing up along with them for the last 6 years and I see so many differences within myself. BTS is a 7-member South Korean Boy Band, Grammy nominated and Billboard Top Hot 1 band who are in the music industry for seven years after debuting in June 13th 2013.

A band which is more like a Family, who are the Music comforters, inspirational individuals for all age groups, who Co- produce songs and convey a message to their fans (A.R.M.Y) and to this whole world, Society. Their lyrics, often focused on personal and social commentary, touch on the themes of mental health, troubles of school-age youth, loss, the journey towards loving oneself, and individualism. Their work features reference to literature and psychological concepts and includes Self love, Finding Happiness and finding oneself with their own Map of the Soul. Their music has been my confidence pill, breaking my wall that i had created myself. Their lyrics literally made me to take up things and stand up without hesitating. Thanks a lot to them i came out of my comfort zones, be it very nervous i wanted to give it a try. From there my journey on self-confidence started. Maybe BTS was a medium through which i started my search for real self and self love, when they started with Love Yourself concept. I was more influenced by the thought of Love yourself. It is a very important concept that made me think so much about myself. The standards that i set myself are always high and higher, and very strict. This really made me to hit myself more when i could also forgive myself for even small mistakes. This was a turning point where i started

addressing myself, my fears, my dreams. This also led to a concept called Map of the Soul – Finding Oneself. I'm still in the journey of my map, though it can't be seen easily, but can be only felt by oneself..

Thanks to their concept "The most beautiful moments in my life" which made me think about what are the beautiful moments that make me happy and my path to search my happiness started. Maybe i started paying more attention to my likes, dislikes and the path to make yourself Happy is in your hands always. I found the key what makes me happy. It can also be found when a person experiences Hardships, having all tastes in life will help you identify what taste "Happiness" has and how delicious it can be. I started to take ownership for my own decisions and really weighed more to my happiness than anything. I would like to thank my Family, BTS, Armys and all my friends who have always been a great support for me. To all those who are reading this, i would like to remind, Love yourself, Find your Happiness.

SARAH DAWN JEBALANCE

Sarah Dawn is a Chennaite, doing her final year MBA in St. Joseph's College of Engineering, OMR. She loves to learn more about God and desires to spread the Joy she receives by knowing Jesus personally to others.

Instagram ID: jebalance_s

WHO IS JESUS?

As we are in Christmas season, let us take a closer look on who Jesus is. In the Bible there is a verse that goes like this,
"And He will be called Wonderful, Counselor, Mighty God, Everlasting Father, Prince of Peace." (Isaiah 9:6)
What do each of these names of Jesus mean?? Let's see. To remember these names with their meanings, let us symbolize each finger of our hand for each name.
1. WONDERFUL (Thumb Finger): Have you noticed that your thumb finger is different and unique from the other fingers?? Yes, our God Jesus is also a unique and a wonderful God. His birth was also unique and wonderful. His plans and His ways are also wonderful and different from what we plan.
2. COUNSELOR (Pointing Finger): Why do we use our pointing finger? One major use of our pointing finger is to give directions to others. Similarly, we need Jesus to direct us in the right way of life. He only is able to give us the right directions.
3. MIGHTY GOD (Middle Finger): What is the speciality about our middle finger? It is the tallest of all the fingers. Yes, Jesus is the greatest of all. He is mighty. He is powerful. He is never ignorant of our smallest issues and never too big to solve our greatest problems. He is all-powerful. He can do anything for you because He loves you so much.
4. EVERLASTING FATHER (Ring Finger): What comes to your mind when you think of ring finger? We put our engagement rings in our ring finger. Do you know why? Because only in that finger there is a nerve that connects with our hearts. So, now you know what I'm going to say. We need to connect our hearts with the heart of Jesus. He is our everlasting Father. The relationship with Jesus is the only relationship that lasts forever. Our earthly fathers might leave us someday, but our heavenly father Jesus will never leave our side, even after our death.

5. PRINCE OF PEACE (Pinky Finger): When you hit a wall or some object with your hand accidentally, which finger gets hurt first?? Yes, it's the pinky finger. Although it is small is size, it aches a lot. Similarly, when you don't have Jesus in your life, the first thing that attacks you is chaos. There will be no peace. But when Jesus enters your hearts, who is the Prince of Peace, He will grant you the peace that is beyond our human understanding. Even when we are surrounded by problems, we can have a sense of peace.

So, now you have a clear picture of who Jesus is and what He desires the most - you!

Have a blessed Christmas and a miracle-filled New Year my dear ones!!

SURANDER S M

Surander is from Chennai doing final year MBA. He loves his family and friends. He is a positive person who thinks about every aspect of life, and keeps positive vibes with people around him. He is obsessed with exploring the world, meeting new people and getting as lost as possible with his loved one.
Instagram ID: surander_sm

LIVE. LOVE. LAUGH

Life is beautiful....only you must know how to balance work with love, laughter and play so as to nurture your body mind and soul. A lot of people out there — hell, all of us at some point — have been so focused on the bigger picture, so intent on reaching some kind of destination that it takes over us completely.
A goal. A dream.
Something that we have been aiming for ever since our hearts were handed our first bow and arrow and told to choose a target. Which is great. It's brilliant to want something so wholeheartedly which becomes your life's mission.
But then it's pretty crappy when that mission becomes your whole life.We've all done it. Been so focused on something big, we completely blur past everything little.
And yet, everything big is a collection of all things little.
Which is why make some time to get happiness from tiny little things which makes your journey filled with love and laugh. Follow your heart. Drive around. Stay a little late. Tick your bucket list. Go on a trip. Get pampered. Make some love. Talk to a stranger. Eat on street. Sleep on roads. Dance in the rain. Write. Trust a stranger. In this process you might fail. You might break. You might get lost. Feel unsafe. You might end up being worst. But you will always learn to lean. Stand strong. Pat your back. Most importantly LIVE. LOVE. LAUGH.

PRIYADHARSHINI KUMAR

Priyadharshini Kumar currently pursuing MBA. An optimistic and ambitious person. Interested in exploring new things and loves to draw comics.

PLAGIARISTIC PEOPLE

Each person is trying hard to follow or plagiaries some one's idea, creativity, style, manners and behavior etc., It starts with a simple way of copying little things like thesis, presentations or papers from websites and making it their own and this in future leads them to plagiaries any work they do. Even when I wanted to think of a topic to finish my write up, I initially thought of browsing in google. People need to put a full stop when this idea of plagiarizing comes into their mind or at a certain period of time, they will get addicted to it. Is plagiarizing and getting addicted to it is such a crime? Yes, plagiaristic people not only steal others limelight but also other people years of hard work, their dream and life.

SUCCESS TURNS INTO CRITICISM

Not only students accused of plagiarism but also famous celebrities, business people and famous artist. Plagiarized people may get success and fame but once their mask is teared all their success turns into criticisms. They will be badly accused by people and all their fame, respect and reputation they have earned even through their hard work so far goes in vain because of their single act of plagiarism. People will tend to think that all their previous efforts and works also might been plagiarized and lose their trust in those plagiarized people.

CREATE YOUR OWN WINGS TO FLY

It is easier to plagiaries but harder to get away with it. In the path of plagiarizing, one fails to create their own path. One needs to understand their true self and create one's own wings to fly. People are gifted with their own talents; it just takes time for them to realize it. Instead of living off others try to find one's own hidden talents and vanish plagiarism.

GUNADHARSHINI C

A girl with lots of confidence and perseverance. A humble and hardworking engineering student.

REAL HAPPINESS OF 2020!

At the starting of 2020,we never had a thought about how this year would be end....

This year is entirely different from all the years, It gave some toughest tasks to human being...some people lost their jobs, someone lost their life, so many people died because of covid-19. When we people went through all the actions happened in this year, people who are all alive are very lucky...

Inspite of being those toughest moments, there is one thing we could clearly watch that were
" humanity ".
Doctors and sweepers worked hard, gave their best! Many people helped others, they provided foods in flood. Whatever it is, if humanity exists in this world, world would be last forever until no one can destroy this world.

In my point of view The real happiness of 2020:

* humanity increased among the people.

*I have spent lot of time with my family, I helped lot to my mom..

* I can help some poor people nearby me....

May the 2021 will give all the happiness to all the people and the upcoming year will make poverty less, healthy life to all the people

My new year wishes in advance!!!!

LUCYA IMMACULATE M

Lucy is born in Chennai and residing in Ennore. She is doing her 12th grade in our lady's higher secondary school. She is an average student and she loves to sing ,dance ,writing poems ,act and to play violin. She is a person who loves to be loved. She want to be a light in the darkness, hope in the despair, a sparkle that can start a fire. She want to break the barriers that separate people from each other. She profoundly believes that love can change the world. She loves to touch people's heart and comfort them. She want to be the change to create a better world.

Instagram ID: luz_287311

THE BLUE RAYS OF HOPE

The blue rays of hope is a short story to light up the frozen hearts. Once there was a chick fell into a grave. Everyday became a nightmare for the young bird. All she heard is her echoing footsteps and all she saw is darkness. She battled with her fears and tears every day. She waited for her death until one day she saw the first light of the dawn. A sparkle of hope lighted up her frozen heart and she gave up to give up .she believed that tomorrow will be different but also questioned herself what she's gonna do today to make a different tomorrow. The day came to reveal the truth about her. She flew out and she realised that she isn't a chick of some other bird but an eagle's. She is an eagle who was a born fighter. Now she became the only target of thousands of arrows and millions of swords. But she is bravely diving into the clouds of fire and taking the arrows straight to her chest cause she is an eagle whose wings is made of diamonds. Pain is what that builds her

Are you gonna be a chick forever or are you gonna realise that you are an eagle ?

JANANI KANNAN

Janani is an open minded person with a strong sense of right or wrong. She strives to bring out social struggles through her stories. She is passionate about technology and is an avid reader. She has currently settled in Chennai working as a software developer. She is particularly fond of dogs.

Instagram ID: jann_cent

ONE HATE STORY

I walked hurriedly towards the marriage hall and I glared at the short muscled man beside me who was responsible for this delay without which we would have returned home by now. We walked in silence. Only a blind as well as a stupid would have willingly married this irritating fool. Love must be truly blind to bestow this fate upon me. Two years now and it was enough. I was going to open up to him about the divorce papers I have in my purse tonight. One last act as an happy couple and then it's done. No more false smiles, puffed eyes and dampened hopes. Today, it's over. We found a spot to sit in the crowd. Few moments later a deep rumbling shook the entire structure and parts of the ceiling broke down. Everyone crouched down to prevent being hurt by fall. Finally, it came to a stop. Then chaos broke... Everyone rushed towards the exit and another rumbling much worse than before shook the structure. The chandelier above us dangled and fell. The crowd beneath moved sideways. I was pushed to the farther side of the wall away from the exit losing sight of him. I searched for him and found him on the other side of the chandelier motioning me towards the exit. I rushed towards the exit when a deep crack spread on the floor and from it came fire like hell itself. The hall broke in half as if it were a toothpick. I toppled over and hit the wall with a clank. The fire was blazing hot raising to the ceiling. The broken half of the hall now rested on the roof below. There was no way that I could reach the exit now. Few men had broken the window and climbed out onto the roof. I heard my husband's voice frantically calling out for me and I shouted back assuring him that I have a way out through the window telling him to take the exit. Few left on this side climbed out onto the roof not knowing what else to do. Firemen had arrived and had propelled a ladder for us. I looked up to find that another wave was passing through the building and a major portion of the building including the hall

and the roof where I stood moments before collapsed down. I knew that no one could have escaped this not even a head strong arrogant irritating short muscled man. And with that realisation my world went blank. A tight knot formed in my chest and spread throughout my body. My vision blurred to indistinguishable colours and the voices died down. Memories flashed.. Then there was nothing. I searched deep and found nothing. I found no reason to move... to speak... to live... Something heavy pressed against my left side. A stink floated in the air. I realized something and found the strength to turn. I found a short muscled man covered in dirt, debris and soot sitting beside me. He was heaving heavily as if he had run a marathon. "I saw someone ugly sitting here ..I know then that I had found you", he said grinning. I glared at him. As a tight knot in my chest loosened, my world came back. Then I knew, to expect to feel love always was imagination and so was life with no fights and hate. Happily forever is a lie. To hate and love is life. I was happy that I had a life ...with him!

HARITHA BASKAR

Haritha Baskar is born in Tamil Nadu and settled in Chennai, currently pursuing MBA. She is a jovial and friendly character who loves nature . She is passionate about playing Table Tennis .She is a person who is concerned about mother earth and its protection. She likes to write contents rarely. She loves to explore and learn new things. She also loves to help people.

EMBARRASSMENT TO A NEW BEGINNING

Embarrassed? Does it actually trigger our insight? YES, but most of us think of it as a disgrace. In my opinion, embarrassment is faced from the day we step out of our home say it can be school, college, workplace. But many think it makes them dejected. Some people lose self-confidence and make them discouraged. In my perspective, people should actually learn from what they go through.

Some things are easier to evoke, and some are easier to disremember. I can remember my most embarrassing moment as if it happened in the recent past. I've tried, over the years, to forget this moment, but it just never seems to go away. As I've gotten older, I can think back to that day and just laugh.

I was 12 years old when I experienced this kind of circumstance. I was asked to join summer camp, there, many did not bring their lunch including me as we thought it will be provided. So, the teacher generally informed "Bring your own plates" in front of the class. The next day mostly everyone in the class brought their lunch but I just took a plate and went to the class. The teacher did not have any good impression of me as I mistook the whole sentence because, at that age, I was not very good at English. Many made fun of me. At that age, I was not comfortable and it was not easy to get through this kind of situation.

I immediately asked my mother regarding this and she made me take the situation in a positive manner. I was advised to develop my knowledge in English and with the help of this wise lady, I started working on how to develop my skills in English and here I am writing this article. Therefore, you need to think of aspects that can make you feel pleased, honored, satisfied, proud, and gratified.

OVIYAPRIYA K

Oviya is a 23 years young girl who is doing her MBA. She loves to be in a fantasy world and thus she wants to share her thoughts and innovation to her friends too.
Instagram ID: fan_of_dora

POSITIVITY

Positivity? Yea.... it is..!!

So, where is it? When it ll come? How to attract it? Okeyyy... My dear reader.. just comfort yourself...!! Let me take you, people, to a colourful world of positivity.....!!

Once there was a very big tree with lots and lots of beautiful butterflies. Those butterflies have many-hued wings. Their coloured wings are the colour-constructive element to the tree. On a holy morning, every butterfly was celebrating colours with their loved ones. The tree looked even more colourful that day. At this time of celebration, a new butterfly came out of a pupa. The new butterfly named Mitta was very cute with random colours in her body, but.... she was made with uncoloured wings. She doesn't want this to happen. She was very depressed due to her un-coloured wings. With a very sorrowed face and mind, she was searching for her friend Hitta who was with her during the caterpillar stage. Suddenly Mitta's heart beats with joy. Her eyes started shedding tears that came out automatically due to extreme happiness. Why? Yes, she saw her friend Hitta! They hugged each other expressing their love. Hitta greeted, "Welcome Mitta" with a bouquet. But Hitta noticed that Mitta was not that happy. "What happened Mitta?", she questioned. Mitta replied, "I am born with uncoloured wings. So I can't fly anymore". Mitta strongly believed that the one which has colourful wings could fly. Hitta told to give her a try. But she can't. Mitta's wings didn't permit her to go up. Hitta patted Mitta and said, "Dear, this is a common problem that every butterfly faces. Your wings will become coloured by tomorrow morning". Mitta was very happy about this. She ran around with happiness and hope, believing that the next day would be colourful.

The next day morning while Mitta woke up, She was very surprised to see her colourful wings. She cried out of joy. She tried to fly this time because she got her own coloured wings.

She tried with happiness and finally after several attempts, she started flying. Hitta and Mitta started flying from Mountain to mountain and Tree to tree. They didn't leave any place uncovered. Finally, it is a rainy time. All other butterflies stayed under a tree but Hitta and Mitta enjoyed it. When the rain stopped, Mitta started noticing that her colourful wings were fading due to rain water. "Why? Anything went wrong here?", Mitta exclaimed. Hitta replied with a smile, "Mitta, this is your real wings. Yesterday night, I have coloured your wings". "But why?", Mitta asked with her tearful eyes. "Dear, you believed your colourful wings and started trying with hope and positivity. Finally, you flew. But actually the coloured wings did nothing to your self-trust. You believed and you worked. That's it...!

With positive hope and a supporting environment, we can hit the Sun and challenge the Moon...!!

ANJALI GAUR

Anjali Gaur is a 19-year-old history honours student from Daulat Ram College Delhi University. A polity enthusiast she is a passionate speaker who loves to read and write about current world happenings. she loves exploring Indian art and architecture. A prodigy, she is a multi-tasker who loves to explore every avenue of life. A social worker she thinks that changes comes when we connect to the roots. For her writing is her life, it has always been her escape from the real world. It's an essential part of her existence. She quotes that the best gift for her is a diary and pen.

Instagram ID: ekbaatbatau._

FROM POSITIVITY TO PRACTICALITY

After getting into all these tough years of teenage. I got to know the importance of self-introspection and getting to know what's in your shoes. It all began in 2017 when I lost entire control over my senses. And soon that pressure became a subtle part of my life. I know it's being continuously preached in our minds that sometimes the things are not into our hands but I think it is partially true. Because what we do make things and when we don't do it then the entire picture changes. Maybe the result is not in our hands but we can control our actions. Then amidst all the, One day I realised that why I was doing all this to me when the only loss was mine Then after days of wondering, I came up with this idea known as 9 days of changing life. For me, these were the 9 days of introspection. I decided to introspect my own life for 9 days and came up with some of the amazing realizations . We ask ourselves to be positive, in every condition and then one day when nothing works out we somehow have to end everything and the same goes with the equation of life as well. When we don't talk about the toxicity we carry, then we will never be able to remove that from our life.

So the first step is to accept things and then after analysing them try to find out a practical way to move on. Being optimistic motivates you in every situation but being practical helps you in judging the right consequences and making you ready for things in a prior manner. But then is it possible to be practical without being positive? Answer to this is no, and, indeed, you can't be practical without being positive but then you shouldn't be positive about the results, leave that part on practicality, Judge things wisely and be ready for what life offers. That is the true art of winning life. Don't hesitate to talk to someone at that moment if talking about things helps you in solving and provide you with a little happiness. Then do it and if not then, do not waste your time on unnecessary people!

They can never get into your shoes. You alone have to fight and be your own master.

While reading a movie review I came across one dialogue that "Har ek insaan ka Apna sky hota hai" (Every person has their sky)

I realised that life goals are very personal, the sufferings, the achievements are very personal and at the same time some people must be important for you but then it's your life. No outer force should regulate it. It's your life in the same manner, not every sky is blue, not every dream is the same, not every life is the same. Paint your sky with your colours, paint your life in your way. Have control upon your words, actions, toxicity, positivity, dreams, ambitions. Stay positive with your deeds and think about the result in a practical way that will not only save you but make you a strong person. So find positivity in practicality.

Flairs and Glairs, a platform by a student for the students. We are esteemed youth struggling to carve out our path for our future and we follow a basic mindset Since everyone is not born with all-round skills. Joining hands with people who are born to execute it with perfection is the best way to evolve. Self-Evolution is the need of the hour but, evolving as a community is what we strive for. The initiative as kickstarted by, Founder- Mr. Shubham Shah with the motive to utilize the skillset and talent of writing has now a team of 10+ people who are actively participating into newer forms of learning and discovering talents among youngsters. We Provide platform and services like Publishing opportunities, Open mics, Workshops, Hands-on training. Operating with Brand Name of Flairs and Glairs (Publication House), we offer the chance of elevating a passionate writer to an esteemed author With Brand name Teekhe Zasbaaat. We bring to you an opportunity to get accustomed with the Public Speaking and Presenting of Thoughts along with regular challenges to brush up your inking spirit. The newest initiative to extend our services we introduced in a new writing Platform- The Glittering Fables and Ink Over Tears.

We Choose to Fly Like A Falcon than to be a

Leg Pulling Crab.

To Know More: Infoline – 7781900870
Mail Us At-
flairsandglairs@gmail.com / info@flairsandglairs.in
Or Visit is at
www.flairsandglairs.com / www.flairsandglairs.in
Social Handles- @flairsandglairs @teekhezasbaaat

www.ingramcontent.com/pod-product-compliance
Lightning Source LLC
Chambersburg PA
CBHW071754150726
47998CB00005B/1928

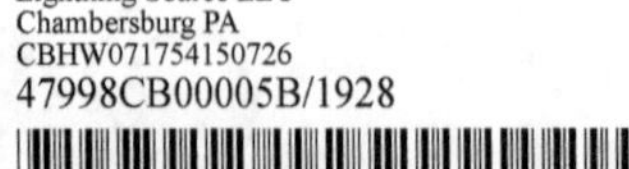